Second Chances

J.L. LEMON

ISBN-13: 978-0-6151-7041-1

Published 2007 by Up At Midnight Publishing
www.geocities.com/upatmidnightpublishing

For my parents who provide endless love and support. Thank you both.

1

The phone was going to ring again. Sydney felt her sister growing more anxious with each second. Sam would devise a reason for calling, of course, despite the fact they covered every subject known to humankind during Sydney's move from Savannah. All she wanted was bread, milk and a new toaster considering her old one fritzed out in a unique, albeit frightening manner. After the sparks and smoke cleared, she vowed to spend a couple of extra bucks on a better brand.

Sydney glanced at her Camaro's clock. If Sam didn't hurry, she'd be late for her usual phone call. Today's conversation would be shorter than normal since Sydney's ability to reason vacated the premises. Before leaving the apartment, she forgot her coat and now roamed downtown Atlanta in jeans and a hunter green sweatshirt. The attire was usually suitable for late autumn but not the icebox encompassing the city the last week.

She moved her cell phone closer to her hip. Sydney classified her sister as a textbook worrier. People would pay her to worry for them and she'd do justice by them, giving them their money's worth. For the past few days, Sam fretted about Sydney's move back to Atlanta. The crime, the traffic, finding a safe apartment in a decent part of town, the cost of that safe apartment, the people she'd interact with... "You just never know" was Samantha's attitude.

Sydney never truly understood the sheer volume of worries there were in life – probably because her sister relieved her of such burdens and agonized over them on her behalf.

Her sister proved correct on one important subject. Travis Shaw. He was something to worry about. Sydney fell for his charm and unwitting smile only to languish emotionally because of his runaway mouth. Had she known Travis suffered from a debilitating case of superiority complex, his days in her life would have been numbered. Sydney's highly anticipated promotion to senior editor at Fantasy Publishing, a romantica publisher, registered as a mere yawn with her boyfriend. Once he learned she accepted the job in Atlanta, he laughed, saying, "What they need is an FBI raid, not to promote women to a higher degree of immorality."

With that, she snatched his Wall Street Journal, whacked him upside the head with it and ordered him out. Logan Calhoun never would have insulted her job – or her. He prided himself on being a gentleman and Sydney could vow he was.

Logan had it all, good looks, a strong muscled body and a courteous style. A man any girl's mother would love for a son-in-law. *Now that hurt*, Sydney flinched.

He and his brother Ethan seemed to compete for her attention, Ethan in a blatant manner, Logan in his reserved, poised way. She'd fallen for Ethan's playfulness, she supposed. Plus they shared the same grade through school while Logan was two years ahead of them. She simply felt more comfortable with Ethan, she supposed, even with his juvenile behavior. Logan, on the other hand, let her know throughout school he liked her but never infringed on hers and Ethan's relationship – until Ethan slept with Amanda Lewis less than two weeks after proposing to Sydney. Logan's reserved facade cracked and a startling tempest rose from inside. He'd lashed out at Ethan for betraying her then, as though merely looking at her tamed him, he held and consoled her. He then politely asked for a chance to win her heart. Polite – that was Logan.

Sydney drove down I-75 South, deciding to grab a bite somewhere, probably at Burger King. On second thought, probably not. A sandwich sounded better. Actually, she just wasn't hungry. The recollection of Logan's devastated expression filled her brain. She'd crushed him with one word – no. At the time she meant it. No more Calhouns.

After finding Ethan in bed with Amanda, she'd turned and run. She wanted to run and hide forever but Logan literally caught her as she ran away. Landing squarely in his brother's embrace, she welcomed Logan's soothing voice, his gentle touch. Even his kiss. After his tender kiss, he declared his feelings for her and promised never to betray her trust as Ethan had, made promises to her for love, protection, loyalty and more. Then she said it. The mere sound of the word launched him into a verbal rage beyond her wildest dreams. To emphasize his fury, he punched a tree. Twice. She'd run home with Logan trailing her, still pleading with her. She'd yelled at him to go home, to leave her alone and he finally had.

After Samantha learned about Ethan's indiscretion and Logan's presumptuousness, she packed Sydney off to Savannah to stay with her friends. After only a week, she found the job working in the mailroom of the smaller division of Fantasy Publishing. After a while, they moved her up the ladder until she held the title Junior Editor. More than pleased with her life on that scale, she slowly forgot the embarrassment of her youth and carved out a new life. But she never forgot Logan Calhoun, the man who declared his love for her – and she rejected him. The longer she stayed in Savannah, the more he lingered in her mind. The more she wanted to call and apologize but common sense told her otherwise. Logan would never forgive her for refusing him. She hurt him too deeply.

Sydney vowed to look up Mr. Calhoun in the directory. If he still lived in Atlanta, she'd debate whether to get in touch. If he was married now, she could salve her conscience. If he wasn't, well, chances were he wouldn't want a part of her anyway.

Traveling through Atlanta equaled revisiting her past. It was extremely unpleasant for many reasons, she prayed for it to end quickly and vowed to resort to anything short of violence to make it happen.

She cruised along at a respectable twenty miles an hour with more than an occasional drop to fifteen or ten. At this time of day, hardly anyone drove sixty-five on Atlanta's expressways but this verged on ridiculous. Sydney expected bicycles, tricycles and turtles to pass her by.

The drive was longer and slower than she was accustomed to but she lived in Atlanta now, not sweet, laid-back Savannah, where life seemed unhurried and easier. Certainly *closer*, a point not lost on Sydney the past few days.

Her thoughts broke with a sudden jangling of her cell phone. Sam, as usual, was right on time but if Sydney heard "Chain of Fools" once more that day, she'd scream. Next on her list – change the ringtone to something ominous like "Tubular Bells" or "Halloween" because every time it rang, she wanted to hurt somebody.

She swept her hair over her shoulder. The thick loose waves draped far below her shoulders and tangling with it, her sister and the move to Atlanta proved nearly too much. For a moment, she entertained scheduling an appointment to whack off half her hair's length then decided she shouldn't waste the money. Sam's phone calls would push her to pull it entirely out by the roots.

The phone kept ringing and Sydney rolled her eyes. For the past few days her sister's worry scale tilted in the red zone causing Sam's dialing finger more exercise than necessary. Without fail, Sydney expected a call every three hours. Finally after an eleven o'clock call at night, Samantha finally and mercifully went to bed. But straight up seven in the a.m., the jangling on the night stand proved Sam was up and around and worried again.

Curling a wayward strand of hair behind her ear, she answered the phone, "Hi, Sam."

"I'm that obvious?" Not giving Sydney a chance to answer, she inquired, "How's the move going?"

Sydney shook her head. She'd spent the earlier part of the week between Savannah and Atlanta, moving belongings and leaving behind a beautiful, sedate city. By midweek, she visited her new office for introductions with her new co-workers. Today was the first day she dedicated to setting up housekeeping, a fact that clearly escaped her sister despite their dozens of conversations, "Told you yesterday I was finished traveling, Sam. No more trips to Savannah."

"Good. The roads aren't safe for women anymore. All manner of terrible things happen these days."

"I know," she slowed for a gentle turn then sped up to enter the expressway. "You explained most of them yesterday with exceptional detail. I'm *okay*, Samantha. I promise."

"Can't stop me from worrying. How far is your office from home?"

"I forgot my yard stick so I don't know. I'll be safe though."

Sam's tone firmed, "You're too cavalier about this, Sydney. Women are attacked every day in large cities." Then, "What are you doing?"

Bracing her knee under the steering wheel, she scratched her head, "Trying to drive while assuring you. Not an easy task, believe me."

As though Sydney hadn't replied, Samantha rattled off a schedule, "I'm free next Wednesday so I'll check out your apartment, the surroundings and I want to see your office. We'll do a walk-through on security and –"

"Sam, *I'm* not free next Wednesday. I have to start work this week." Sydney looked in the rearview mirror and noticed the red and blue lightbar flashing behind her. *Oh great...*

"I'll drop by for your apartment key. I'll let myself in and fix us some dinner. You don't mind –"

"I gotta go. I'll talk to you later." She hung up, hearing her sister still chattering as she did. Then she turned off the cell phone so Sam's call back wouldn't interrupt her new predicament. After all, police officers frowned on interruptions while issuing citations.

This was just her luck. Less than a week in Atlanta and she was pulled over for speeding. If her sister didn't insist on hovering, this might not have happened. If Sydney thought ignoring the persistent calls might work, she'd have done it. But knowing Sam, she'd alert the National Guard and Marines that she hadn't answered the scheduled three hour check call.

Sydney hoped this wasn't a precursor of things to come. Sneering at the cop car behind her, Sydney angled the Camaro to the curb, cursing her stupidity and bad fortune. Two miles back the speedometer read 65 and the speed limit read 45. After killing the engine, she began digging into her purse for license and insurance.

"Step out of the car please, ma'am," a male voice directed.

The demand caught her short. It was a routine stop, wasn't it? So why ask her to get out, especially in this weather? Still gutting through her purse, she answered, "Officer, I realize I was speeding..."

"Ma'am, step out of the car *now*."

"Well, *okay*." She fisted her license and insurance knowing eventually he'd want that too.

The chill in the air bit into her skin. The sweatshirt provided little protection from the humid, bitter breeze blowing across her, making her wish she'd at least worn a jacket.

The door swung wide and she swiveled to stand up. Her vision followed the uniformed legs to see a young, skinny officer, his hands shaking just slightly. Initially she pegged him as cold, like her, but then saw he wore a thick duty jacket. Then it hit her. He was a rookie. Officer Brooks wiped his brow while trying to hold his composure, "I'll need your license and insurance."

Sydney rolled her eyes and nearly smiled. It would be a cinch to talk her way out of this ticket. A little charm, a sassy smile thrown in for good measure. It usually worked with veteran cops in Savannah so this rookie was no sweat. The kid could barely hold his clipboard steady. He advised her to stay put, which wasn't entirely difficult given the bitter cold. At this rate, she'd freeze to the damn car before he figured out she was clean of outstanding violations. She crossed her arms, watching him amble back to his car. Then she spied another cop in the passenger's seat. This officer was no rookie. He also looked none too pleased to be with a rookie either. At first glance, he appeared to be in his early thirties like she and large in frame considering his shoulders crowded his entire half of the seat. Without wanting to appear obvious, she looked away.

After what seemed forever, she heard a car door. It was the partner. Her initial judgment was correct. He definitely looked seasoned in his work. *Okay, I get a ticket. I'll just cram it in the seat and pay it later. No big deal.*

Sydney's vision dropped but her arms stayed crossed. Two large feet encased in perfectly polished black shoes filled her vision and she followed them up his legs, his veritable tree trunk thighs and higher. God, he was tall. Her head inclined to meet his scrutinizing gaze. She felt, for lack of a better word, little.

Behind the intimidating glare, he was gorgeously handsome. Short dark hair, killer brown eyes and a body to die for. As fine as he looked, he still was a cop. A cop who'd probably delight in citing a new resident. Atlanta – the city of bad memories.

His voice backed up his size, "Sixty in a forty-five zone, reckless driving, talking on a cell phone while driving and topping it all off, no seat belt. I advise you to rethink your expression, Ms. Eatonton."

Surprised by his bluntness, she answered, "I apologize, Officer. I was on my way to–"

"Don't throw excuses at me," his patronizing tone warned. "That and your pretty looks may have worked in Savannah, but it doesn't cut it here."

Still utterly stunned, all she managed was, "Excuse me?"

"Your record from Chatham County. You've kept their department well funded with all your infractions. Can I hope for the same for our fair city? I could use a raise."

Now that was enough, "Pardon me, Officer, but is it common practice to talk to people like this?"

A smug, nearly malicious grin appeared, "How much do you want me to forget this citation?"

Sydney stared blankly a moment then searched for his name. The insinuation of his statement, the confident wink he gave her, the mere bizarre nature of this encounter rattled her beyond words. To top it off, he'd removed his name tag. This wasn't shaping up to be a good day at all. More than ever she wished she hadn't turned off her cell phone. A call from Sam sounded damn good right now since this nameless cop made predatory moves toward her. He leaned in, "Ask yourself what you'd do not to have this citation."

Sydney pressed back against the cold car window for space, "I think I'd rather deal with Officer Brooks."

He placed his hand on the car next to her shoulder, closed in, "He's unavailable. You're dealing with me."

He was close enough she felt his heat and smelled the spicy scent of his aftershave - and his desire. His pupils dilated around their dark brown rims, turning his eyes nearly black. Whatever he intended to do, she was not willing to go through with it. Her quickening breaths created clouds of fog, showing every degree of her nervousness, "Officer, please step away from me. I'm sure this is against department policy."

His lips neared hers, "Leaning?"

"Intimidating citizens." Her hand raised slightly as his body moved closer. She placed her hand firmly against his chest to punctuate her feelings.

The demand was simple, deep, and strangely quiet, "Hands at your sides, Ms. Eatonton."

Sydney didn't move. She mustered a swell of courage, although she was freezing due to weather and nerves, "No. I'm uncomfortable with your position and your conduct. They are both inappropriate."

The show of attitude merely spurred him on, "You're one step away from being arrested. You're resisting a police officer." He withdrew his handcuffs and dangled them in front of her, "But with a little encouragement I could make your arrest very pleasurable."

If she could possibly be any more offended, she didn't know how.

Sydney leaned back to see if Officer Brooks watched. Unfortunately, his nose was buried in paperwork in the cruiser. *Great. So that's how they do it here.* The large cop jingled the cuffs again as he leaned against her ear, "You used to be adventurous, Sydney. Have you changed that much?"

The words jolted her and she faced him, their lips only inches apart. In those few seconds, he'd moved even closer, the length of his body aligning with hers, touching in places they shouldn't. He knew her but she searched his face for a trace of familiarity. Nothing. Or was there… Those eyes. She recognized those coffee colored pools. Even with the pupils extending over most of the color, she now knew this officer's name by heart. He added another wink for good measure as she stammered, "Ethan?"

"In the flesh, sugar." He nudged against her, "How about that arrest now?"

Her voice instantly froze, "Give me the ticket and let me go."

The frigid response clearly confounded him but only for a second, "Hey, where's the daring girl I used to know?"

She pushed past him now, not caring if she hurt him or not, "She grew up. Either cite me or let me go."

Ethan remained calm, "You're still upset over what happened —"

"Give me a damn ticket or release me."

"Go to dinner with me and I'll forget these infractions, all four of 'em."

She crossed her arms, "I'd eat glass before subjecting myself to eating dinner with you."

Her remark carved his frown deeper, "Okay, young lady. You've sassed me once too often. Turn around."

Sydney's jaw dropped, "You're joking." His hand on her shoulder proved he wasn't. He spun her, braced her against the car, locked one wrist in the cuffs, then the other. "This is how you get your revenge? By arresting me?" She asked, the question not sounding nearly as indignant as she felt. He leaned into her, his chest against her back.

Ethan's lips brushed her left ear, "Last I saw, you got *your* revenge by leaving Atlanta. Well, sugar," he turned her to face him then smiled a mile wide, "welcome home."

2

Officially she wasn't under arrest, at least according to Ethan. It was a cooling down period for her. To Sydney, it equaled being Ethan's pet for a day. No doubt Sam was standing on her head with worry because Sydney missed two calls already. Ethan, however, seemed to enjoy her incarceration. His desk sat across from the cell and he entertained himself by watching her, occasionally asking her questions and when she replied smartly, he reminded her who had the key to the cell.

Throughout her stay, she'd learned the cell was unisex, that women tended to be more vocal than men when locked up and she'd learned that Ethan wasn't a beat cop but a lieutenant. He was riding with Brooks as backup until the rookie's partner returned.

Ethan swaggered proudly around the station, especially around the cell's perimeter. The three working girls locked up with her flaunted their merchandise, cupping their breasts and throwing kisses every time he passed and whistled. What they hadn't evidently noticed was, he whistled at Sydney, not them.

Sydney first became aware of Ethan in third grade when the imp took to pulling her ponytail in class. Sitting behind her, he played all day with her hair, she was convinced, just to annoy her.

By sixth grade, she was convinced Ethan would never mature

intellectually. He was cute but rather childish, mostly because he accepted any dare, the more dangerous the better. Before accepting one, he strutted around, showcasing biceps that were as absent as his rational mind. Sydney just rolled her eyes and told him to grow up. He'd perform the craziest stunts she'd ever witnessed and it scared and angered her, leaving her to walk away shaking her head.

She clearly remembered one dare given by his friends. They challenged him to kiss a girl. On the mouth, they clarified, and not to chicken out and kiss her on the cheek. Placing books in her locker at the time, all Sydney heard the boys say was, "It's gotta be a real kiss."

Not knowing whom they meant, she shook her head, knowing Ethan was on his way to complete the mission. Before she could close her locker, she was spun around, braced against the locker doors and Ethan pressed his lips on hers. Her eyes popped wide as laughter broke out behind Ethan. Then as the kiss lingered, the laughter waned into childlike "oohs". Stunned by his action, Sydney had no clue what to do but wait him out. When he pulled away, he smiled saying, "You taste like oranges."

Sydney remembered her reaction. She shoved him away then rubbed the back of her head, "Ethan Calhoun, the next time you want a kiss, don't push me into the locker."

Ethan's brother witnessed the whole thing, outwardly amused at her dressing down. Arms crossed, the eighth grader appraised his brother visually then turned his sights on the girl rubbing her head.

Logan stepped forward, confident in his stride and intention, "Ethan, this is how you kiss a girl." Towering over Sydney, he watched her swallow hard as her head tipped back. She feared the tall, beefy older Calhoun – a boy who *really* had biceps. As he leaned down, she froze in place, muttering a quiet plea of mercy, "Logan, no."

His thoughtful grin calmed her only slightly. "Yes, Syd," he murmured softly. Framing her face in his hands, his tone settled the sheer fright coursing through her, "Easy, babe. Just remember to breathe."

Her lips parted to object but he held her so tenderly, she couldn't even squeak. Logan descended, his lips on hers, pressing softly at first then firmer, encouraging her to open further. When his tongue eased into her mouth she jerked with surprise. Good grief, her first kiss - as unexpected and brief as it was - was only minutes old and it was pretty good by her standards. But this second kiss nearly floored her. *Breathe, Syd.* How did Logan know she'd forget to breathe? Sydney half-heartedly turned away only for Logan to follow. His hands cupping her face refused her to part until he was ready. His touch had been gentle, non-threatening. As his tongue explored her mouth, she'd ultimately settled into the kiss, learning the movements, twirling her tongue and sliding it together with his. Suddenly, Logan shoved her harshly into the wall, breaking the kiss entirely. Then she discovered Logan hadn't pushed her, Ethan had shoved his brother and pounded on his back, yelling at him to get away from her. Sydney had never seen Ethan so angry. His face beet red, his fists swinging wildly, his voice growling. Logan appeared barely affected by the attack as he looked into her wistful green eyes, "You do taste like oranges."

High school presented new challenges for her and Ethan. By their senior year, their parents made their opinions known about the young couple. Sydney's mother pointed out Richard Calhoun was a known rounder and his philandering sent his wife to an early grave. She certainly didn't expect any different from Ethan and couldn't bear that Sydney might suffer the fate of marrying an unfaithful man. Meanwhile Richard, during a semi-sober moment, told his son that a life with Sydney would bring nothing but misery while he tried to measure up to the Eatonton's expectations. The Eatontons were considered wealthy, at least wealthier than the Calhouns, but it never occurred to either Sydney or Ethan that their relationship would cause such an outrage.

Sydney abandoned reminiscing for a deep sigh. Watching Ethan meander through the police station, hearing his laugh, brought back so many memories. His large, well-muscled body filled the uniform perfectly. It made her wonder why he decided on police work, considering his father spent a lot of time exactly where she sat. Between the drunken fights and sober ones, she was surprised either Calhoun boy grew up gentle. Both Logan and Ethan were the most tenderhearted men she'd ever known. Ethan's sweet nature, his need and desire to please her made her fall in love with him. And back then she fell hard.

The cell was colder than she expected. She seriously considered accepting the jacket Ethan offered earlier. For now though, she rubbed her hands together to warm up a little. Ethan strolled by and Sydney unconsciously stroked her left ring finger, remembering how delicate Ethan's engagement ring felt on it. It wasn't extravagant, just a small diamond set in white gold but it meant everything to her. He presented it one night at dinner and it took all of three seconds to accept. That night they celebrated their engagement by going to a motel and making love all night into the early morning. She'd likely never live that stunt down, not with her parents, not with Samantha.

Less than a week later, she decided her family was right. When she'd walked in on Ethan and Amanda, they were in bed asleep, both stark naked. Amanda cuddled Ethan close, her hand resting on his chest, her leg flung gracelessly across his thighs. Sydney couldn't remember what woke them unless her crying had. Logan said she screamed but all she honestly recalled was throwing the ring at Ethan, hitting her target and trying to find the fastest way out of the Calhoun house. Logan, evidently clueless to the scene in Ethan's bedroom, had let her in that morning. When he saw her blazing through the house, he grabbed her into his embrace to settle her down.

Now, leaning against the cell's concrete wall, Sydney repeatedly thumped the back of her head against it in a fruitless attempt to block the painful images. The memories stung as hard now as they had for sixteen years. Seeing Ethan only added salt in her wounds but she couldn't drag her vision from him. He strolled to the bars holding a soft drink, "Want a soda? It's your favorite."

"Well, that depends," she answered calmly. "Because the question is, do you want to *wear* it because I'm not thirsty, Ethan. I just want out of here."

He shook his head with a grin, "Threatening a police officer is a serious offense."

Lolling her head to face him, she scoffed, "Oh, I'm sure you've been threatened with more ominous objects than a Diet 7-Up."

The women padded up to Ethan, reaching for the soda. Ethan withdrew it, "You girls will be outta here soon enough. You can get your own."

"And you're keeping me here indefinitely?" Sydney asked in an incredulous tone. "You know, I could file charges on you, Ethan. False imprisonment."

"Not a wise thought."

She crossed one knee over the other and folded her hands in her lap, "Why not?"

Ethan smiled and waved a piece of paper like a trophy, "Because I know where you live. Unless you want me on your porch day and night, you'll think twice about filing any charges."

"You dog," she groaned. "How did you find out? I haven't even been in town a week."

"Modesty forbids me to boast but I am a cop, sugar. You had papers in your purse from Fantasy Publishers so I called and got your address."

Sydney scrambled to her feet and grabbed the cell bars. Anger heated her better than any jacket possibly could, "You called my employer? That's great, Ethan. I just got that promotion and now—"

"Easy, babe. I didn't tell them you were a jailbird. I told them who I was and that I heard you were back in town. Must be my charm but few people refuse this lieutenant." He batted his eyelashes, "It helped when I explained how close you and I were before you left." He blew her a kiss, "Here's to our long awaited reunion."

And I'm the one locked up, she thought.   Sydney stood

unimpressed, "Does the Atlanta PD know they have a psychotic on the force?"

Ethan swung the cell key back and forth, "Want to see this anytime soon?"

"I'm allowed a phone call, you know," she reminded.

Grinning nefariously, he shook his head, "Our special guests aren't. Now, if you want to visit central booking, I can arrange that phone call. Otherwise, you're all mine."

Ethan knew she didn't want to make the arrest official but sitting behind bars was driving her nuts. She watched him thumb through a stack of papers that looked vaguely familiar to her, "What are you reading?"

"Something I found in your car. Oh, the car is being towed to your apartment, by the way."

"How chivalrous of you. Not making me walk all the way to the interstate to fetch it. Do you mind not reading private material?"

"Did you write this? Had I known you had these fantasies back then, whoa, baby."

Sydney flopped back onto the bench, "If you'd do the ethical thing and close the manuscript, you'd see someone else wrote it. I'm the assistant editor."

Ethan read another paragraph while taking a sip of coffee. His eyes bugged, "Holy Mother of God. This stuff reads like porn." He sat the cup down absently, his attention riveted to the page, "Damn good porn, though."

She ran her fingers through her hair, sighing, "I can die happy now. Ethan approves."

He rose from his desk, manuscript in hand. Uh-oh… Sydney didn't know what he planned but the cell was far from empty. The three other women with her appeared very keen on their conversation.

Ethan held the manuscript so she could read the print, "So, like here," he pointed to a paragraph, "when you read that, does it ever affect you? Y'know, start your engine?"

Suddenly she felt extra participants in their discussion. Peering to the side, she saw the three women huddling behind her to read. A faint "ooh" rose near her right shoulder. The paragraph in question was old news to Sydney. She'd already read it and re-read it. And yes, it did affect her heavily. "My engine is just fine and doesn't require assistance starting. Not that it's any of your business."

He leaned in, his voice low and sexy, "It used to be my business. Like for it to be again."

Sydney tried to reign in her anger. Despite her attempt, she lashed out in frustration, "You're kidding. You gave up that right when you…" She noticed the women's interest heightened with her show of anger so she toned down her reprimand, "You know when."

"Temper, temper, Ms. Eatonton. I see that hasn't changed either. Behave, sugar, or I'll be forced to reenact pages 48-52." He pushed the manuscript through the bars for her to read. She didn't have to. The words branded themselves in her memory.

The male character sated himself on the female until basically rendering her cross-eyed and unconscious. The countless different positions read more like the Joy of Sex but there were enough steamy scenes that any woman would break a sweat just reading it. In fact, Sydney debated about keeping the intense scene in the book. She classified the material as borderline for Fantasy Publishers. She flagged the pages with a Post-It note and intended to ask the senior editor's opinion. Evidently Ethan thought she liked the scene so much she bookmarked it. It was impressive and powerful but reenacting the scene with Ethan was farthest from her mind. She'd actually pictured Logan and herself. And, her vindictive brain taunted, that's why they called it a *fantasy* because barring a miracle, Logan wouldn't be caught in the same room with her.

She felt the heat in her cheeks before he saw it, "Can you please let me out of here? You've made your point."

Ethan looked at his watch, "Well, whaddya know. My shift is about over." He faced her, mentally judging his options, "I'll release you if you give me a kiss."

"Oh, get over yourself," she grumbled. He really thought a lot of himself these days.

He leaned closer to the bars, "Listen to me, sugar. I'm letting you go without that citation. That should count for something since it saves on insurance costs. So what's a simple kiss going to put you back?"

About sixteen heartbreaking years... Then she thought again. Yeah, she could do this. All he wanted was a kiss? She'd make it a kiss on the cheek. That was benign enough. "You've got a deal."

Ethan grinned in childlike glee. Sliding the key in, he twisted it and opened the door. Sydney stepped out and puckered up for the platonic kiss only for him to stop her, "Not here. Hold on a minute."

He made the rounds saying goodnight to all and gathered her belongings. He refused to hand over her purse until they were outside.

They stepped into the cool early evening air and Sydney paused a moment then kissed him on the cheek, "There. Your kiss." She tucked her purse under her arm and began marching away to search for a cab.

Ethan took her arm, "Whoa there. Freedom means more than a peck on the cheek. Give me a real kiss."

"You never said anything about what kind of kiss. Let me go, Ethan."

He frowned into her angered features, "You're pissed at me for something that happened years ago. Can't you give me another chance?"

"Stop it already." She tried to free her arm but he didn't release her. Ethan nudged her against the cold brick of the station wall. His lips descended to hers. She turned before they met. She spent hours sitting on a hard bench inside a cold jail cell and he wanted to kiss her? He *had* to be joking. She threw the only curve she knew, "How's Logan?"

He kissed her cheek but at the mention of his brother, his lips firmed and he pulled back, "He's fine. Why?"

"What's he doing now? Does he still live here?"

Ignoring the questions, he murmured nearly pleadingly, "Let me kiss you."

Realizing no answer would come, she inquired, "Will you let me go then?"

"Take a chance." He leaned in again and she didn't turn away as their lips met. Memories of similar moments flooded her mind. The times when she craved this kiss. The time she drew him from his slumber into a kiss very much like this one. The time after they'd made love.

Ethan's hand dropped to her waist and she felt his cool touch on her skin. His tongue urged her to open for him. His efforts were met with failure as she broke the kiss. Breath mingled and frosted in the cold December air as they stared into each other's eyes. She recognized the hunger in his expression. Breaking the physical contact seemed her only salvation. Except his hand still rested on her waist in a familiar way – like it belonged there. The tickle of his fingers tried to draw a smile from her. It was all too much too soon. Finally she mumbled distantly, "Take me home."

3

Ethan wanted to slug himself and shake sense into her. He'd quietly driven her home, taking only enough time to make chitchat and tell her he was happy to see her again. By her reaction, she believed him but didn't really want to. During the trip to her apartment, he memorized every part of her possible. Besides being wrapped in his duty jacket, she looked exactly like she had when she left. The most gorgeous woman he'd ever seen or wanted. The long waves of chestnut hair cascading past her breasts, breasts he remembered very well. As well as how she reacted to his touch. Her eyes haunted him day and night for years. Those emerald pools and their intimacy, their adoring expressiveness as she looked at him. At least back then. Now they could slice him to ribbons with one glance. Her voice always turned him on. It was a low sultry tone that made him want to jump her every minute of the day.

He'd spent most of the day with a partial hard-on. He hadn't immediately recognized her that morning. Only when Brooks brought her license back to run it through the computer did it hit him. Sydney Eatonton. The name sprung his attention and erection to new heights. She was back in Atlanta. For how long, he didn't know but he intended to take full advantage of the opportunity. He watched her from the cruiser, leaned against the red, late model Camaro, arms crossed and tapping her left foot impatiently. Brooks seemed relieved when Ethan took over, saying he knew her and not to panic no matter what happened.

Seeing her surprised indignation as he snapped the cuffs on her made riding with Brooks, possibly the most inept rookie known to man, the most worthwhile decision he'd made.

Ever since he'd met her in grade school, Ethan knew she was the one for him. She'd been there either with him or in his dreams, keeping him sane. Growing up with a drunk, carousing father hadn't been easy. With no constant female influence to temper him, he'd had plenty of rough edges, especially about the finer points of women. If it weren't for Logan guiding and instructing him, he'd have wandered through adolescence clueless. His older brother filled in as surrogate father, teaching Ethan about life, love and sex. He was a great teacher but early on Ethan had a serious gripe. Don't teach Sydney as well. He'd stated that rule when Logan tongue-kissed Sydney when she was in sixth grade.

Then there was Syd. Even at his craziest moments, she still hung around him, defending him, making him feel accepted. He screwed up more than a guy should ever be allowed, especially with her.

Ethan laid on the bed, shaking his head. Acting the consummate jerk seemed part of his genetic makeup. Maybe he was like his father. Plenty of people told him so. The incident with Amanda only reinforced their opinion of him. He regretted the moment he laid eyes on Amanda, much less sleeping with her. She'd always hung around him, kissing and making advances while Sydney remained more reserved. He hadn't pressed Sydney to sleep with him, well not too much, but once they got engaged, she'd given him a taste of what heaven could be. Amanda, however, always eagerly invited him to her, especially since his engagement. The one time he'd brought her home, he knew his only obstacle was Logan who was already in bed at the time. Ethan considered it his bachelor party. After all, every man had one last fling before getting married, didn't they?

Before he realized it, she was on top of him doing things Sydney probably never imagined a woman could do. Things a lady like her wouldn't dream of doing.

When he awoke, it was to a scream and to Amanda wrapped around him, naked. His vision met Sydney's horrified expression. Both he and Amanda were uncovered, he on his back, she on her side, her head snuggled under his arm and hand on his chest. Her bent leg draped over his thighs, presenting Sydney with an obscene view of Amanda's goods.

He sat up, basically throwing Amanda aside, "Syd, this isn't what you think," he managed to say before getting clocked with the engagement ring. He cursed as the small diamond plinked him on the bridge of the nose then tumbled into the bed covers. Ethan frantically dug through the sheets until finding the ring, the one bond to Sydney he intended to salvage. She would marry him, damn it, all he needed was a few minutes to explain. She'd listen and understand. Sydney always understood. But his gut warned him of the worst. He'd slept with another woman while engaged to her. Women weren't likely to forgive those indiscretions.

She bolted from the doorway as he fought Amanda's sleepy attempts to keep him in bed. The ring secure on his pinkie finger, he leapt from the bed, calling for her. He heard her crying and his heart twisted with hurt and fear. He had to catch her and try to explain. It was a stupid mistake, one that would never happen again. But what began as a secret affair now had two extra players. Sydney and Logan. He heard both voices in the living room.

By the time he reached them, Logan had her in a tight embrace with her twisting to free herself. He threw Ethan a scathing glare, "What the hell did you do?"

Ignoring his brother's accusing tone, he begged, "Syd, please don't break up with me. It wasn't anything. She doesn't mean anything to me."

"Who?" Logan fought to keep her within his embrace, "Damn it, Sydney, *calm down.*" He gnashed his teeth, intensifying his fierce frown at Ethan who whispered Amanda's name. Without further explanation, Logan grew to furious proportions, "That *slut?*" Then he gathered Sydney outside, keeping Ethan at bay, "Get some clothes on, stupid, and stay out of Sydney's sight. And mine, while you're at it."

Ethan grabbed a blanket from the couch and wrapped it around himself. He followed them outside, "Sydney, baby, it was one night and it won't happen again, I promise. Please," his voice broke while extending the ring, "take the ring and wear it. *Please.*" Ethan never felt so desperate in his life. He hadn't thought that... Well, he just hadn't thought period. Now Sydney remained tucked in Logan's embrace and wouldn't look at Ethan for a second. His brother comforted her, holding her tenderly as she cried.

Ethan heard her whisper something to Logan who shifted his vision to him, "You really want to know what she said?"

Ethan hadn't but nodded anyway. Logan squeezed her tight, "She said you can shove your ring."

Bringing himself back to the present, Ethan spared himself the entire torment of that moment. He did remember Sydney packed up and left in one day. How could a person leave town that fast? He tried to track her down for the longest but got nowhere. Her parents nor Samantha folded on her location. Now she was back and he would reclaim her as his.

Ethan toyed with this idea all night. He needed to force her into a date with him. Once they straightened out the past, they'd get on with their lives together. He took a drink of bourbon to bolster his confidence. She'd fight him, he knew that. But now she fought on his territory instead of hers in Savannah. While she was in Atlanta, she stood no chance of winning. Eventually her name would be Calhoun.

Lifting the receiver, his index finger methodically dialed Sydney's cell number. It rang twice and she answered. He didn't know how to begin the conversation except, "Hey, did I wake you?"

Sydney sounded amazingly awake, "No. Spending the day in jail has a way of curtailing the concept of sleep." She sighed, "Ethan, it's nearly one in the morning. What do you want?"

"To apologize for throwing you in the pokey. I just didn't want you to run off again."

"I have a job here. Hard to ignore that."

"True but I want to make it up to you."

"You didn't file the citation, that's good enough for me."

"Not for me. Go to dinner with me tomorrow. It's my day off."

"Lucky me but I'm supposed to turn in the manuscript tomorrow. That means I have to work."

"I'll pick you up after work. I know where the place is."

"Ethan, the answer is no. Now I need to try and steal a little sleep if possible."

Frustration took over. This new, more independent Sydney confused him to the point of exasperation. She used to listen to him. She used to do what he said within reason. Now everything he mentioned met a fixed blockade. He masked the aggravation with a firm response, "I let you go once. I'm not making the same mistake twice. Get some sleep and I'll talk to you later."

"Good-bye, Ethan." Sydney hung up in his ear. What he said was true and he fully intended to keep that promise. If it killed him, he'd change her mind about him.

4

Sydney trudged through the doors of Fantasy Publishing bleary-eyed and tired. She'd squeezed four hours sleep out of the night and fully intended to reach her quota tonight. She wouldn't meet Ethan for dinner but go to bed early instead. Reaching for the door, she was surprised when it opened for her and the doorman greeted her – surprisingly by her name. The elderly gentleman reminded her of her grandfather. Attired in perfectly pressed pinstripe gray, he tipped his cap to her, greeting her in a soft-spoken Georgia accent while opening the door for her. The Savannah office didn't even have a doorstop, much less a friendly doorman.

The home office was nearly imposing compared to the one in Savannah. The twelve story glass building was dolled up with purple neon lettering along the top of the building that announced "Fantasy Publishing". Even the pink and purple awning broadcast the name as it flapped in the gentle breeze.

Years ago, Sydney figured she'd be relegated to a secretary's job in some lawyer's office. Not that that was a bad job but Savannah's job market certainly wasn't Atlanta's. Never in her wildest dreams did she imagine herself walking in this building as senior assistant editor for the company. As a teenager she'd read the books Fantasy printed. Every month she scoured the bookshelves at the neighborhood store, delighted to find the newest romances of the month. Now, instead of straight romance, they dared into more erotic writing but Sydney still enjoyed reading the submissions and living vicariously through the characters.

She strode by the board announcing employees and their office locations. Surprisingly she saw her own name already added. "Senior Assistant Editor, Sydney Eatonton, 10th Floor, Suite 12." A satisfied grin emerged while she angled toward the elevators. The elegance of the entire building staggered her. Their signature color was purple but everything from the carpet and walls were accented with pinks and golds. The elevators exuded opulence themselves. Dark paneled walls with thick pin-stripe gold ribs enhanced the rich wood color. The door itself a solid mirror of gold with floor numbers highlighted in script.

Her office was enormous compared to the one in Savannah. Her desk was mahogany, worn in just the right places to indicate a working desk and not a trophy. The black leather chair positioned behind the heavy desk made the room daunting yet impressive. On the desk sat an up-to-date computer as well as her nameplate – the latter being first thing she brought in with her. The clamshell color walls and burgundy carpet made the room comfortable, at least to her.

The staff seemed friendly enough since she'd been there. A little family, in fact. Rose, a woman in her early twenties with flaming red hair, emerald eyes and a line of freckles across her nose acted as receptionist. If one didn't recognize Rose by her uplifting tone of voice, they were sure to locate her by the bright, cheerful wardrobe. Lime green, hot pink and neon orange seemed to suit her well.

Sydney classified Rose as cute and peppy by nature. She always had a smile to share and was so comfortable with Sydney that she asked her to escort her to the hospital for an MRI later that week. Sydney agreed, realizing that medical tests presented worries all their own and no one should be alone during them.

Jason Butler, Sydney's new assistant, had to be the friendliest young man she'd ever known. Less than five minutes of knowing her, he began calling her "honey" and "darling" and felt comfortable enough to hug her on sight. Dressed in navy slacks and a robin's egg blue oxford, Jason looked to be about twenty-three with short blond hair and clear blue eyes. With his animated gesturing, a delicate gold hoop in his right ear glinted in the light like a twinkling star. He flitted around Sydney like a butterfly around a flower, staying only long enough to gather then fluttered off only to return for more work later.

His only awkward moment came when he announced he was homosexual. He volunteered it, he said, because his last boss made his life hell from the second she found out. He needed to know if his lifestyle presented a problem with Sydney.

"Are you good at your job?" she'd asked. In return, he'd nodded. She extended her hand, "That's all I need to know." Jason, being Jason, pawed her hand aside and grabbed her in a bear hug. Then he proceeded to rattle off a list of higher-ups to beware of, who brown-nosed, and who would cut her throat merely to get her job. When Sydney began taking notes, he stopped her with a soft touch to her wrist, "Honey, here's the list," he said handing her a sheet of paper. "Just make sure to memorize it. This business should be called Peyton Place, not Fantasy Publishing."

Rounding the corner, Sydney halted at the sight of Rose's suddenly beaming expression.

"Good morning, Sydney," Rose called. "You look a little tired, sweetie. Didn't get any sleep?"

Sydney glanced at her, sensing something dire. The redhead quirked her brow knowingly – about what, Sydney didn't know but she smiled guardedly in return, "Not much, no. I, uh, had a long day yesterday."

"I can only imagine." Rose fanned herself as she flushed red.

The action stopped Sydney, "Rose, is something wrong?"

"No, sweetie, not at all," she winked.

Odd, she thought while ambling to her office. The moment she passed Jason he stood, "Sydney, darling. You certainly look tired today."

"Okay, joke's over." She sighed, "What is everyone talking about?"

Jason brushed her forearm lightly, "Oh, honey, it's okay to tell me. You can tell me everything. Anything. I'm like Fort Knox. I'll keep it safe."

Sydney realized Jason's lifestyle was different from hers but *everyone* acted out of character, even him. Tell him what? He evidently wanted to tease her more, "I understand you have your own welcoming committee. He sounds dreamy, darling."

Crap. Double crap. Ethan struck again. It was in regard to the address request and she knew it. "I know he called for my address, Jason.

And," she cut him off before he spoke, "we are not as close as he led you to believe."

"Oh, but honey, what he told me about you…"

Sydney panicked. No telling what Ethan spouted in a moment of ego. She sat the manuscript down along with her purse. The pained feeling spread to her expression, "What did he say?" *No, scratch that.* She *really* didn't want to know. Before she could retract her question, Jason leaned closer, "Let's just say he's got it bad."

"As far as I'm concerned, he can keep it too." Just as quickly, she grabbed her purse and the manuscript and headed to her office with Jason immediately behind her.

The instant she rounded the corner to her office, she regretted coming to work. What she saw astounded her. The giggling behind her came from two people, at least. Jason and Rose and God knew who else. "Honey, he's in love with you," Jason chirped.

Sydney stared at the arrangement of red roses positioned in the middle of her desk. The desk she'd barely sat behind ten minutes since being in Atlanta. The crystal vase held a good dozen, maybe more. And to think the whole Ethan scenario began with a craving for toast. Some called it destiny – she preferred to call it a blight. A touch on her shoulder focused her attention on Jason's voice, "Go read the card."

"Or I could just ask everyone in the office what it says," she shot over her shoulder. The inane giggling only worsened so she could only imagine what the card said. Taking the bull by the horns, she marched to the arrangement, plucked the card and read to herself, "I enjoyed yesterday and last night beyond words. Next time I won't use handcuffs.

Welcome back, babe. I've missed you. Ethan."

The blood boiled inside her, beginning in her toes and steadily worked its way up. Her cheeks flamed with embarrassment. Her ears felt like they'd melt off her head. Reinforcing the remainder of her dignity, she placed the card in a drawer and forced herself to face her colleagues, "Okay, the card doesn't mean what you think."

"Of course not, honey," Jason waved her off, obviously appeasing her. "We understand."

Rose also waved it off, "Whatever you do in your private life, sweetie, is your business. However wild and risque," she stepped away trying to stifle a chuckle.

Sydney pushed the manuscript toward Jason, "Do something productive. Take this upstairs, please."

"Yes, ma'am. Right away." Jason started out of the room then turned before leaving, "Darling, he's a hottie."

Sydney settled into her chair, sighing. She wasn't settling for this humiliation at work. She retrieved the directory and looked up his station number, "I need Lieutenant Calhoun's number, please. Sydney Eatonton. Believe me, he knows who I am. Okay, then please leave him a message. Tell him Sydney is declining his invitation. Thanks." She hung up. She just wouldn't be there when he arrived to pick her up. There was more than one way to fix this problem.

For what seemed an hour, Sydney stared at the name and phone number. Taking the plunge, she'd looked up Logan's name in the directory. The list of Calhouns extended a whole column and into another. But there was only one Logan T. Calhoun among them. According to his listing, he lived in a very upscale area of town – not quite Buckhead but its stature in Atlanta was admired all the same. Certainly nothing in the realm of the squatty little apartment she currently rented.

She'd reached for the phone six times already, managing only to dial the first four numbers before chickening out. This time, though, she'd follow through. All he could do was refuse her offer to meet for coffee. Which, in turn, would break her heart and make them both even, she supposed. Stopping briefly to utter a prayer for success, she reached for the phone once more, "Don't say no, don't say no…" she whispered while methodically pushing the buttons. Sydney smiled when she passed the fourth number in Logan's home phone. The butterflies in her stomach kicked into overdrive when she passed the fifth and with the sixth, her hand began to tremble. What did he sound like now? A deep voice, like Ethan's, only deeper. In her dreams, he'd answer the phone happy to hear from her after so long a time. In reality, she figured she'd be lucky if he picked up the phone or called her back.

She closed her eyes and took a deep breath to brace herself for the final number. Finger poised over the "2", she opened her eyes and nearly screamed. Jason stood directly in front of her desk holding a small package. Cutting her a sideways glance, he inquired, "Are you trying some kind of Transendental thing? Meditation by phone or something?"

Dropping the receiver in its cradle, she leaned forward covering her face with her hands. Accepting momentary defeat, she replied, "No, I'm trying something called Personal Purgatory where I pay for my past sins forever. Only masochists are successful at it so I should pass with flying colors."

An empathetic smile crossed his features, "Well, maybe this will brighten your day. It's a special delivery for you, dropped off only moments ago."

"Unless it's a ticket letting me off the Ethan Express, I formally decline."

The mention of Ethan's name lifted his mood, "Maybe it *is* from Hottie."

"Stop calling him that." She studied the package closely, weighing it in her hand as she took it from her assistant. It felt somewhat heavy. It was wrapped in thick brown paper similar to a grocery bag with her name and office location printed in blue ink. Below, in red ink, read "URGENT".

She ripped into the package, much to Jason's pleasure. The contents fell into her lap with a jingle. Jason strained around the desk to see, "Oh my,"

With one finger, Sydney lifted the handcuffs carefully as though they dripped with slime. Then she opened the small note attached, "Don't make me use these again. I will see you tonight or next time I'll leave you locked up."

Jason suddenly howled with laughter. Sydney called him down, "Don't breathe a word to anyone about this. I mean it. I've had enough of this guy already." She dropped the cuffs out of sight in her desk drawer while vowing to leave work so late only owls and bats were roaming about. Ethan would go to dinner alone. Just as she had for so many years.

5

Sydney glanced at her watch. Eight thirty. Surely Ethan gave up waiting on her. She dreaded sneaking out of the office like a thief but he left her no choice. She wanted to go home to a peaceful meal. Gathering up her new manuscript, purse and those tacky handcuffs, she strolled confidently down the hallway to reception. Turning the corner, she startled at the sight of two large male legs, one crossed over the other's knee.

"Hello, Syd. I see you got my gift." Ethan was leaned back with a magazine propped open in his lap. He closed the book and tossed it on the table, "Is the work here that engrossing? I should quit the department and come to work for you."

Her hand settled over her heart in a futile attempt to calm the frantic pounding. He'd scared her to death. Drawing a shaky breath, she answered, "You don't want to work for me."

He rose to his feet, overshadowing her by several inches. Being alone in the office with him moving in made her nervous, particularly with his ravenous expression.

Ethan gathered the handcuffs from her. She heard them jingle and saw the metal glint as he played them between his hands. The devilish tilt of his chin cautioned her to step back as he spoke, "Think about it. You'd be my boss and I'd have to do everything you said. 'Yes ma'am, Ms. Eatonton, anything you say, ma'am.' Doesn't it sound intriguing?"

"Not really," was the wary reply. She remembered this look from their engagement night. The look he displayed just before jumping her.

She took another step back, seeing him swing the metal bracelets provocatively.

Countering her move, he angled closer, a mischievous grin curled his lips, "So you're probably more the opposite."

"Opposite?" She asked while backing away again.

"The kind that doesn't give orders. The kind that *takes* them." Just as he finished he snapped a cuff around her left wrist. "Gotcha, babe."

The metal unyieldingly clicked into place, efficiently subduing her. Ethan executed the move with deadly precision, giving her no time to react. When she finally realized her predicament, she jerked on her arm, hoping to free herself, "Damn it, Ethan. Not again."

"I told you, sugar. You try to escape me and I'll lock you up." He wrapped the other bracelet around his right wrist.

Sydney groaned again. Weariness and hunger ravaged her from head to toe, "I have work to do. Unlock these things and let me go."

While tugging at her wrist, he allowed a playful yet evil laugh surface, "Come along, my pretty captive. We're doing some serious discussing while you're at my mercy."

Disbelief temporarily diffused her anger, "You've slipped a cog,

Ethan. You can't just kidnap me."

"It's not kidnapping. I told flibbertygibbet you'd be out a day or two."

"Flibbertygibbet?" Her brow furrowed as she struggled to catch up to him.

Ethan gently tugged her faster, "The girl up front."

"Rose. Her name is Rose." She stumbled into the elevator, grateful his frantic pace briefly ceased, "In case you're blind as well as clinically insane, I'm shorter than you so either let me go or take smaller steps." Loud hunger pains punctuated her tirade, prompting Ethan to pat her stomach, "First on our list is to satisfy your current hunger."

"Then give me a baseball bat and two minutes with you in a dark alley. That should do it because you've obviously got a brick for a brain. *Let me go.*"

"No chance. I've got you and not wasting a minute."

Sydney struggled to catch up, struggled not to lose her belongings. The new manuscript threatened to flop out of her hold and the anxious trot they'd developed dislodged her purse somewhat, "I'm not going anywhere with you like this. I look like a criminal."

Ethan kept a steady pace to his Camry, and to lessen her embarrassment, took her by the hand. She wrapped hers around his – at least now she didn't look like a fugitive led by handcuffs.

Streaking past her Camaro, she voiced her utmost displeasure about leaving it. That car, she gladly informed him, cost her a fortune and if anything happened to it there would be hell to pay. Ethan agreed to have a patrol car swing by occasionally to check on it. Still not happy but still being dragged along, Sydney watched the red SS Coupe grow further from her protective sight then they suddenly stopped.

Ethan opened the Camry's passenger door, got in then deftly angled his large frame over the protruding gearshift to the driver's side. His free hand grabbed the steering wheel for leverage and he wrenched himself effortlessly into his seat. Sydney marveled at his acrobatic abilities, "Witnessing your skill makes me wonder how many women you've carted off in this particular fashion."

"Only you, sugar. You in?"

"Uh, *no*." Her shackled hand braced against the gearshift panel and she swung her legs in. After she closed the door, he started the engine and smiled. Ethan shifted into Reverse then First gear. Sydney's hand followed in unison with his shifting. Debating over letting her hand flop or bring the situation to his attention, the decision was made when he lifted his hand to the steering wheel, effectively putting her arm in a strain. "Ethan," she griped, "I'm sort of attached here. Do you mind?"

"Sorry." He brought his hand down and clasped hers. "It's my first time abducting my true love."

"I'm not your true love so stop it." She watched the traffic fly by as he wove in and out of cars and buses. The ride reminded her of the Mind Bender at Six Flags over Georgia. The three loop rollercoaster zipped along its rails at fifty mph. Sydney's current ride now exceeded sixty mph down International Boulevard. Christmas lights flashed by at warp speed and she tightened her grip on his hand, "I do have family that would appreciate seeing me in one piece instead of dangling from the branches of fifteen live oaks or smashed flat against the CNN building. Slow down."

He snorted, "I'm a cop, Syd. I know how to drive."

That was certainly debatable, especially when the car suddenly sailed sharply to the right. Sydney cringed, her lips uttering a silent prayer for sanity to reunite with common sense. Then, "Just because they put airbags in the car doesn't mean you have to use them. Wherever we're going, we'll actually get there if you slow down."

To appease her, he slowed the car to fifty but she still braced herself for the next turn. Sydney tried to occupy her fear by watching families with shopping bags and children jumping gleefully as they exited toy stores. Children. She'd thought about having kids once but the idea left when she moved to Savannah. She threw herself into her work, dedicating every free moment to proofreading and editing manuscripts other women had written. Other people's dreams and fantasies. It was voyeuristic in some ways. Seeing into other women's imaginations but it temporarily diverted her desires of a husband and children. The times she allowed herself to think of them, Logan Calhoun entered her mind then her heart ached all over again. For a moment, she thought about asking Ethan about his brother then feared the inquiry might cause a major accident. Ethan remained painfully focused on driving through traffic – and driving her positively crazy. The following left turn assured her she'd made the right choice. Grasping the door handle with a death grip, she knew mentioning Logan would surely cause disaster.

6

"Do you even have a key for these things?" Sydney's first words after stepping in his apartment left him speechless. Good enough for him, she thought. The ride, along with bone weary hunger, left her plagued with constant nausea.

His hands perched on his hips, "Yes, sweetheart, I have a key. It's in my shorts. I figured it was safest there since that's the last place you want to be."

Her vision lowered to his crotch. Great. He was cunning if nothing else. "In your *shorts*? What'd you do, sew it in there or tuck it between things?"

Ethan chuckled, "Why don't you find out?"

A moment of silence passed, her sights still on the target. Then, "You still wear boxers?"

Was she seriously considering taking on this treasure hunt? She saw his body react to the thought of her hands trolling in his shorts. The space in his shorts now grew smaller as his erection became evident. He swallowed hard and eked out a "Yeah." Obviously he wondered the same thing. Would she dare try for the key?

Sydney balanced her options. No matter when she searched, if she did, he'd get the wrong idea. But she really needed out of his apartment before old memories overwhelmed her.

"I really want the key, Ethan."

"Tell you what. Let's eat dinner and see how things go. By then hopefully you'll change your mind and want to stay."

"Oh, like I want to stay handcuffed to you forever."

He shrugged with a smile, "Well, modesty forbids me to assume..."

Indignation engulfed her, "Get over yourself, Ethan Calhoun. I just want free of you, once and for all."

Her defiant stance clenched his jaw again for a different reason. He loathed her independent spirit and always had, "If I have to steel reinforce my jeans, you won't get that key until I'm ready." He tugged her through the living room to the kitchen. The hodgepodge of furniture didn't surprise her. Ethan always possessed eccentric or disorganized taste. She preferred to call him eccentric despite the fact he truly was the latter.

A worn chest of drawers from the 1940's sat next to an old brown recliner. The circa 1970's side table seemed rather small on top but the cubbyhole beneath provided room for old issues of the Atlanta Journal-Constitution, an empty beer can and the antiquated carcass of a Snickers bar. Sydney's first thought was of Samantha. Had her sister seen the table's contents, they'd have heard her scream in Alabama. She would have also had kittens over the Penthouse magazine lying on top of the table next to the TV remote.

Stepping past the Art Deco coffee table, Sydney saw two beer cans, three issues of Sports Illustrated, two Playboys, and a National Geographic. She nearly choked upon sight of the last but figured somewhere in the folds lay a naked woman or Ethan wouldn't own it.

The tan carpet ended at the kitchen entrance which switched to robin's egg blue linoleum reminiscent of the 1950's. The fridge, table and chairs looked fresh from June and Ward Cleaver's house. The aqua Formica top showcased by shiny metal legs shouted Leave It To Beaver louder than anything in the apartment.

Ethan saw her looking around, "The place, well, the kitchen, came like this. Pretty retro. The living room and bedroom are all my stuff." He opened the small fridge and searched for sandwich makings. In his right hand, he grabbed both the bologna and cheese. Sydney spied the mustard and took it in her left. Ethan's free hand snagged two cans of Budweiser, "It isn't Atlanta's finest but it'll do. We could have had dinner at a nice restaurant if you hadn't tried to weasel out of our date."

"A date conjured in your imagination. I declined the invitation." She glanced around the cabinets, "Where's the bread?"

He opened an upper cabinet and retrieved half a loaf. It hit the table with a resounding thud. Sydney's nose wrinkled as she poked it. Instead of sinking into the loaf, her finger met something akin to petrified wood in a plastic wrapper, "Did this come with the apartment too?"

Sneering, he opened the bread and laid out enough for their

sandwiches, "I haven't died from eating it yet." With silent determination, he began whipping together dinner. As though from memory, he slathered mustard on the bread and added two slices of bologna. Then he handed it to her, "Mustard with bologna. You're weird, Syd."

"This coming from a man who handcuffs women to himself so they can't leave."

He smirked while preparing his sandwich, "Worked, didn't it?"

They sat next to each other at the table. Sydney warily examined her sandwich. She tapped the corner against the saucer and winced at the solid sound, "So did the Edsel but no one said it was a good idea."

"You enjoy harassing me, don't you?"

"As much as you enjoyed arresting me, yes." Sydney held the sandwich in her left hand, Ethan held his in his right and they lifted their hands in unison. Their lips came within kissing distance and both stopped. Sydney quickly bit into the sandwich before he acted on the idea of kissing her. She pulled her left hand down just as he tried to bite into his meal. The click of teeth and a muted moan nearly made her smile. "Syd," he admonished gently, "I have to eat too."

"Should have thought of that when you handcuffed me to your dominant hand."

He waited for her to take another bite then grabbed the links on the handcuffs, holding her hand completely still while he took a bite of his. "You've always been feisty," he forced the words between the mouthful of food.

Sydney waited. Surely there was more to his announcement than that. He chased the food with a two gulps of beer, "Even in bed. That's what I love about you."

She flushed red as her gut twisted. Of all the things he remembered about her, it was that. She refrained from furthering his observation but he quite happily proceeded, "I remember that night so well."

"You should forget that night. We aren't the same people we were in high school."

"Your smile, that's what I recall best. That sleepy grin beaming down at me until you fell asleep, your head resting so perfectly on my chest. I stroked your hair for an hour, I know. Never wanting to let you go."

The words flowed from his lips like it was yesterday. The inflection and sentiment behind them made her pause from her meal. She wasn't sure she could handle where he was headed with this monologue. By the next sentence, she was positive she couldn't.

"I still love you," he said.

Her dinner soured instantly. Bantering back and forth with him was one thing. Talking about their past was entirely different. The hurt of Amanda Lewis finding her way in his bed flooded back so hard it nearly drowned her. She stood up, "Ethan, I really have to get home."

He urged her into the chair by the wrist, "I know you hate me for what happened but you never let me explain it."

"That's because I don't want to hear it. You slept with her, end of story." She reached for his jeans, desperate to get away from him before reliving the events that drove her to Savannah. She couldn't deal with revisiting it anymore. Her fingers nailed his belt like lightning again but struggled with the buttons of his Levi's.

Ethan covered her hand with his. Sydney closed her eyes, willing the image of his erection from her mind. He was stiff as a board under the denim. Dealing with his hard-on was much easier than dealing with his stubborn attempts to explain his indiscretions. He gently squeezed her hand, "I'm sorry I slept with her. I've been sorry for sixteen years."

Sydney, still leaned across his lap, looked up at him. His hand moved to her cheek, stroking it lightly as he gazed down at her. Ethan lowered his lips to hers. A tender sweep, a request for more.

Flashes of Logan entered her mind, caressing her as they inevitably did. The sweetness of his manner, the tender way he held her to a kiss. As though he'd die the moment their lips separated. "My precious Syd" he'd called her, mere moments before she broke his heart. Oh, how she wanted to be his precious Syd again.

That thought alone broke the beginnings of Ethan's kiss. He appeared stunned to realize he was the only eager participant of a longer, more meaningful kiss. He blinked and mentally tried to refocus, "Sugar, what's wrong?"

"I can't do this, Ethan. Please unlock the cuffs. It's not like I'm going to run away. My car is still at work and I need to get home."

Resigned, he stood prompting her to her feet as well then unzipped his fly.

"You really have the key in there?" Sydney's skepticism flared in full force.

"Now why else would I be digging in here in front of you? Yes, it's in here."

And, from what she saw, he had a bitch of a time working around his erection to find it too. Finally, he unbuttoned his pants for a roomier search.

"Have you found it yet?" She inquired.

His shoulders drooped, "No, Syd, not yet. If you're so antsy to leave, why don't you look for it?"

She shook her head, "It's safer if I stand over here."

He heaved an arduous breath and let his hand wander into his shorts once more. The longer he searched, the more worried he seemed to grow. Sydney sensed it, "Having a problem or having too much fun in there?" His withering glance sobered her instantly, "You don't have the key?"

"Houston, we have a problem," he answered with a look of near despair.

"Are you joking or are you just trying to get me in your shorts?"

"No, I'm not joking but sure, if this will get you in my shorts, feel free. Look for the key, Syd. I can't feel it anywhere."

"I'm not getting in there, Ethan. You have two hands, get with it."

"Okay, but you're coming along for the ride." He yanked his jeans straight down, surprising her. She bent practically double as the denim slid to his ankles. Ethan toed his shoes off and stepped out of his pants. Sydney searched the pockets, hoping he'd lied to her and kept the key in there instead of his boxers. Just as her hand reached forward, he tugged her back up. He took his shorts and slid them to his ankles.

Sydney gasped quietly at his nudity and turned away for modesty's sake – his and hers.

"Didja suddenly get shy? We'll never find it with you staring at my coffee table," he tugged her around to face him.

Keeping her vision trained down, she focused on his boxer shor… "Happy faces?"

"Don't say a word. I had hopes of a different kind of evening with you."

Tongue in cheek, she peered at his blushing cheeks, "What more could you ask for, Ethan? I'm handcuffed to you, you've lost the key and now you're naked from the waist down."

He snorted. "You're not."

"And I won't be either." She dipped to her knees and began searching the shorts for the key. Ethan remained standing, watching her poke around his shorts while on her knees. Her brow lowered, "Ethan…" she warned. "Get down here now."

He sank to his knees but she'd already searched his clothes. No key. They both stood on all fours silently staring at the pile of clothes. Then she eyeballed him critically, "Nice trick but it won't work." Her voice rose from its sultry depths to a louder, more determined tone, "Get me out of these now."

Sheepishly, he grinned, "Sweetheart, I was going to but I lost the key. Honest to God, I had the damn thing right here," he fumbled through the shorts and displayed the small condom pocket. "It must have fallen out at some point."

Sitting back, Sydney rested her palms on her knees, "Okay then, where's your other set? Every cop should have a backup set of cuffs and keys. Where's *that* key?"

Ethan cleared his throat uneasily. Nothing need be said at that point. She blew out a breath, "Then find someone with a key."

"My partner comes back from vacation tomorrow. We have to wait until then."

"He's the only cop on the Atlanta PD with a handcuff key?"

Ethan turned incredulous, "Do you honestly want me to call a uniform out here? I mean, look at us. Let's just wait until –"

"Tomorrow. I can't deal with you until tomorrow. Look at you."

His arousal reacted when she looked at it and Ethan merely smiled, "It's not like I meant for this to happen. Although fate does have a way of –"

"You call this fate. This, Ethan Calhoun, is equivalent to hell. Now I have to sleep in the same bed with you. Something I vowed never to do again."

7

Attempts to turn over met with failure. Ethan pinned her most of the night with one leg over hers and his arm around her waist. His face snuggled so close to her, she felt his warm breath on her neck. This was not how she envisioned her life in Atlanta. Literally chained to her ex-lover.

Sleeping comfortably, or normally, meant surrendering distance. Plus she was a side sleeper, not a back sleeper and tonight forced her into the latter. Ethan, on the other hand, could sleep in any position – and he was an acrobat as well. Without stressing her left hand, he'd managed to side sleep very well except his partial hard-on stared back at her until she threw the blanket over it. She'd refused to remove her jeans just because of his constant aroused state and he refused to put on shorts because of it so covering it seemed the best answer. Plus, there was no need to give him encouragement.

The softness of his bed surrounded her, his scent enveloped her senses, subtly attacking them. An inherent male scent of soap and sandelwood. With every breath she became weaker. It frustrated her that he still had any hold on her emotionally. She'd worked several years to exorcise Ethan Calhoun from her soul. Obviously, she needed a stronger potion or priest.

In the shadowy moonlit room, she stared into the mirrors above Ethan's bed, wondering how she managed to get into this mess. Looking at them both, minus the clothes and handcuffs, it could easily have been sixteen years earlier. Ethan's strong build still eclipsed her in its embrace. Of herself she saw only her hair splayed wildly across the pillow. Cruella DeVil with long hair, she reflected. She looked positively horrible. According to Ethan, however, she looked like an angel.

Ethan's left hand stroked just under her right breast. Sydney thought about objecting but realized he was sound asleep. His breathing even and deep, his lips mere inches from hers. His arm and leg tenderly gathered her closer as though to ensure she remained snug against him. She really wanted to sneer but couldn't bring herself to. Instead, memories of a night spent in his arms crept in. It was too easy to slip into the past, she thought, and too dangerous. Then she thought about Logan, fantasized about feeling his warmth and strength while in his arms. They were seconds away from kissing when the phone rang, bringing her mournfully from the daydream.

The phone continued blaring its electronic harbinger. Instinctively, she reached to answer it when an enormous weight squashed her into the mattress, bringing her to full alert with a loud "oooff". A whispered "sorry" answered her complaint. The instant her eyes opened, she saw Ethan straddling her waist, his still very erect member staring directly at her in the dim light. It pressed tenaciously against her belly as Ethan reached for the phone. She wriggled beneath him, "Ethan, for pity's sake, get off. I'll answer it."

"No, I'll get it." He struggled, his body pitching off balance as he stretched. Quickly, he braced both hands – one on the nightstand, and his bound hand above her head. Her free arm embraced him to steady his movement, "This is silly. Let me answer the phone or we'll both fall to the floor."

His answer was to squeeze his knees into her hips to reinforce his balance on the bed. Now she felt like a mounted horse and all he needed was a Stetson and spurs.

Finally he grabbed the receiver, "Calhoun." A moment passed when, "Do you know what time it is? Logan, I can't go, you know that."

Logan's name brought her wide awake. Had she fought Ethan two seconds longer, she'd have spoken to Logan herself. The possibility scared her and thrilled her at the same time. It also made her tremble beneath Ethan's weight.

He evidently felt her shudder slightly and glanced down, obviously enjoying his position atop her. Sydney also felt his knees locked against her waist, reinforcing their hold. She wriggled under him, "Ethan, get off."

Ethan shifted, trying to stay balanced on her. Inadvertently he leaned forward, allowing his body to confine her further, "Settle down, Syd. I can't exactly move here." He returned to his conversation, "Yes, I said 'Syd'. *That* Sydney, right." His voice suddenly softened, "I'm on top of her at the moment."

"Ethan!" she shrieked. "Don't give him the wrong idea. Nothing is happening because I'm here against my will. He should know that."

She saw Ethan frown at whatever Logan said then, "She's just being difficult right now. She'll come around."

"He needs medication, Logan. He kidnapped me and handcu–" a large hand clamped over her mouth, effectively smothering her outburst. She glared into his warning features with a heat that could melt glass.

Ethan spoke to Logan, "I didn't kidnap her so stop talking prison. She won't press charges." His hand stayed glued over her mouth until he felt her free hand grasp his wrist. She pulled at her bound hand and struggled to writhe from under him – all to no avail. He looked briefly at her, "You won't, will you?"

Before she could slap his hand away, Logan's voice blasted from the phone, surprising them both, "Let her go and leave her alone! That's what she wanted so do it!"

In that instant, Sydney stopped struggling. The weight of Logan's command, the hateful delivery of it, paralyzed every muscle. The realization that he still felt so strongly struck her like a punch in the stomach. It was a good thing, her mind attempted to reason, that she hadn't called Logan earlier. For what it was worth, at least he'd screamed at Ethan and not her.

8

Logan downed the last of his second beer. He seriously considered fetching another but the possibility of a hangover was the last thing he needed. Two was his limit, he reminded himself. He also never drank in the morning but this marked his second before ten o'clock. Calling Ethan and finding Sydney in his bed destroyed any chance of sleep. It also ravaged his conscious mind. Thoughts of her in Ethan's bed choked him with fury. He hadn't intended to shout at Ethan. The words fell carelessly from his tongue, laced with bitterness and resentment. They lashed his brother so deeply it left Ethan speechless. Sydney also remained strangely silent over the phone. Logan uttered an apology then hung up, intent to reclaim the scraps of his dignity and weave it back together somehow. Still, it was easier to apologize for saying *that* rather than, "You screwed your chance, bro. Now Sydney's mine." Logan just had to convince her of it.

Another saving grace of the conversation was Sydney sounded upset to be with Ethan. Strike One on little brother. She remembered Amanda Lewis. As for Ethan needing medication, he probably did. And… Had she said *handcuffed?* Logan shook his head. Knowing

Ethan, yes, he'd temporarily lost his bearings and gone that far off the edge.   Logan felt Sydney was in no direct danger with Ethan – even handcuffed to him – but he'd drive her nuts begging her for another chance.

Logan kicked back on his couch with his feet propped on the coffee table. He switched on a rerun of ER. A good episode should free him of the image of sheer beauty that haunted him day and night for sixteen long years. It would certainly require more than two beers and TV to dislodge the needle from that broken record.

He'd called Ethan later that morning to ferret out details but Ethan refused to disclose much.   Logan felt lucky to find out where Sydney worked and that was merely because his brother basked in gloating about her.   Fantasy Publishing, the kinky romance publisher. Fate couldn't have tossed a better gift in his lap unless it was Sydney herself.

Fantasy's home office stood for over twenty years on Peachtree Avenue.   In the early eighties, Fantasy's books found their way across several student's desks, including his. He and his friends spent countless hours in study hall learning new and interesting ways to please women. Many an hour was spent daring one friend or another to try certain chapters with their girlfriends.

Editing those books wasn't exactly the job Logan imagined Sydney having – not that it bothered him. In fact, he might just want to drop by at some point to say hi. Or he might send a little bouquet to her desk to remind her of him. Flowers served as a friendlier ambassador – more acceptable than shouting over the phone. Logan cringed, praying she hadn't labeled him a loud-mouthed tyrant.

Logan prided himself on self-control. Since childhood he'd had to take over raising Ethan and himself. Their father basically resided in bars or in jail and their mother passed away long before Logan was twelve. He forced himself to rise above everyone's expectations of the Calhoun boys. Nothing or no one made him lose control – except Sydney. She managed to drag out his protective nature, his most basic feral desires and his temper. Staying in control was easy until she entered his life. In junior high, she stirred a feeling in him that he couldn't describe. He just wanted to be with her.

By high school, he'd long figured out what that feeling was. Lust. He found ways to be with her – at lunch or walking her home from school when Ethan wasn't around. Keeping his physical distance, he managed to sneak a few kisses, some hugs and some ravenous glances. After a point, lust gave way to a deeper emotion, one that affected his heart. The times they talked, he found Sydney intriguing, mysterious and thoroughly engaging. They shared stories about themselves and their families – sometimes embellishing wildly to the point they both began laughing at each other. He found her to be a delightful companion, loyal to the bone and a woman he wanted to share his life with – if only she felt the same.

Logan closed his eyes again, recalling the gorgeous eighteen year-old. Eyes, hair, her face, and petite body structure. She hadn't changed a bit, he could tell by her voice. That voice – that sexy ring with just a touch of Georgia accent – depicted pure sexy Sydney. For his sanity, he blocked her from his mind for years. The hurt she brought him by rebuffing him stung even as he revisited the occasion. The old oak tree in their front yard took a helluva beating that day and so did his right hand. His knuckles ached at the memory and Logan blew out a breath and shook out the pain. He chose the wrong time to approach her, he knew that, but the rejection still hurt.

Logan hadn't slept wink that night. Not with her lovely image dancing in his head. And her smile. Nature gifted her with the prettiest smile. Logan remembered in one subtle movement of those beautiful lips, she could swap from playfulness to sinfulness. *The hell with it.* ER didn't faze him so he turned the TV off. What he needed was her beneath *him*, not his brother.

As though propelled by an unseen force, he headed for his computer to check the internet. Once seated, he typed her name in the search query. "Two results found," he read, scrolling down. "Sydney Eatonton, Savannah."

Logan scrolled further down the query page. His eyes bugged at the string of words filling his vision. "Kinky", "Fantasy" and "Sydney Eatonton" all neatly packaged in one fragmented sentence. The query result was disjointed but his mind pieced the words together perfectly causing regions South of the Border to throb with dangerous intensity.

He groaned so pitifully it emerged as a near whimper. Then he clicked on the link. A gloriously colorful intro greeted him. Purple neon letters flashed in sequence, "Fantasy Publishing" then the tag line "Where your wildest fantasies come true."

Seeing a link to the staff, he clicked on that. Nothing in the Atlanta Office. "The Savannah Office," he read aloud, "Junior Editor –

Sydney Eatonton." Scrolling down revealed a staff photo, numbering around fifty, and large enough to clearly show the faces of the smiling employees. It took all of two seconds to lock on her. "Stunning," Logan whispered, awestruck by her image. He swore she hadn't aged a day, as if she'd stepped out of high school and into the business world. Only her attire changed. Leaping from form-fitting 501's to an elegant black silk skirt cut above the knee, a low-cut charcoal blouse accented by an abundance of chestnut waves cascading down her back. Following her curves, he stopped at the black spike heels. Logan's nostrils flared at the sight of her legs. She always had gorgeous, shapely legs.

Logan looked on her left hand. Unlike Ethan who never imaged Sydney with anyone else but himself, Logan knew she was a prize and that men would line up for her hand in marriage. To his relief her hand remained perfectly devoid of a wedding or engagement ring. At the sight, he felt his heart squeeze in his chest before shifting into overdrive – and Logan fell in love for the second time with Sydney Eatonton.

Humans were bizarre creatures, Logan mused. They steered clear of hot stoves once burned but old loves, especially unrequited love, drew them like moths to a flame. Human nature verged on masochism in the purest form. And he, like countless others, would again dive into the familiar, agonizing pattern of precarious passion. The knowledge she remained formally unattached certainly helped drive him deeper.

He entertained thoughts of calling Ethan, asking him to look up Sydney's current address but thought better of it. The call would only fuel Ethan's obsession with her, resulting in a furious race to claim her before Logan did. Though his brother wasn't privy to Logan's admiration, Logan had no doubt Ethan's persistence would rival a rabid wolf if he found out. What his brother forgot was Sydney's mulishness. Neither Calhoun brother ranked highly with her but at least Logan hadn't betrayed her.

He leaned back as thoughts of him and Sydney together filled his brain. He closed his eyes, surrendering to the dream he'd locked away for so many years…

9

"Why is your watch on your left wrist?" Jason extended a fresh cup of coffee as she breezed by his desk. She'd been introduced to Rose's coffee on her first day – a brewed concoction rivaling the viscosity of engine oil and strength of a controlled substance – and vowed to steer clear of it but today she needed a serious caffeine boost. She welcomed Jason's offering but not his question.

Automatically withdrawing her left hand, she took the cup with her right. She tried to look nonchalant but judging by his lifted brow, he'd nearly deduced a somewhat correct image of what happened the night before. She willed away the blush creeping into her cheeks and lied, "Because I was in a hurry this morning. Any messages?"

"Not so far. Then why are you wearing the same clothes you wore yesterday? Running *that* late, were you?" His curiosity rivaled a cat batting a yarn ball around. He wouldn't be happy until the whole thing unraveled into a chaotic mess. While she realized Jason held an unusual interest in her love life, she saw no reason to confirm his assumptions. She'd skirt and fib her way free from them all. "Haven't unpacked all my things yet. Why are you so interested in me today?" She lifted the cup to take a cautious sip. Yep, just as lethal as the first cup she innocently consumed her first day. This time, however, she braced herself. Rose had to be from New Orleans. The city where coffee not only stood on two legs but paraded around on them.

Jason smirked, his blue eyes sparkled, "Oh, honey. I think you're fabulously mysterious. You're barely here a week and you get flowers from an old love, a set of handcuffs and this morning we all noted your car was still here but," he winked, "you were nowhere to be found."

She sipped the coffee tentatively then started the journey to her office, "And no one thought to alert the police, of course."

Jason gleefully leapt to his feet and wrapped his arm around her shoulders, whispering, "But you *were* with Lieutenant Hottie. Tell me, did he take you someplace and make wild, passionate love to you all night?"

A sputtering noise and series of coughs echoed in the hallway, "Heavens, no!" Just the idea horrified her to the point coffee threatened to spew out her nose. She shrugged free of his arm and skittered into her office to hide her cheeks ablaze with color.

Jason eagerly followed, "Something happened. Rose said he sat in reception until she left. Said he seemed restless but very detectively-looking. You come back, same clothes, watch on the wrong wrist. After the handcuff gift, well, you know –"

"And you paid this close attention to Lenore Bailey when she was your boss?" Sydney emphasized "boss" to subtly put him in his place.

Jason merely released the same light, uninhibited laugh as yesterday, "Honey, Lenore was snooze city. You, on the other hand, liven this place. You're mysterious, young, beautiful." Then as quickly he sighed, "Oh, the poor fellow. He must be terribly sexually frustrated right now if you didn't have sex while he had you in handcuffs, I mean."

Her businesslike tone intensified, "We did not have sex and I wasn't in handcuffs. Now cut it out."

He shrugged, "Then you'll wear your watch on your right wrist, lefty."

She threw a scathing glare in his direction, watching him smile again, "Gotcha."

Pointing to the door, Sydney dropped the words like boulders, "Go... To... Work."

Jason chuckled while heading out the door. Pursing her lips, she planted herself in the soft leather chair. It wrapped around her much like Ethan's bed had. She took a deep, calming breath. Ethan's scent filled her senses, bringing her attention back to the evening they shared. He hadn't been entirely obnoxious, she reflected, and that surprised her.

A soft knock on the door broke the dream. Turning, she saw a woman standing in the doorway. They'd met days ago but she couldn't place the name. All she remembered was "aloof with a high, nearly irritating voice". Impeccably dressed in a designer suit, her blonde hair impeccably twisted in a tight bun, the woman waited then flashed a rather impeccable smile. As though sensing Sydney's loss of memory, she introduced herself again, "Ms. Eatonton? I'm Cynthia Andrews from Public Relations. Were you notified of Friday's event?"

Smoothing a few wayward strands of hair, she laughed quietly, "I've barely been notified I'm awake. What's happening Friday?"

Suddenly Cynthia blossomed into a flurry of movement toward her. Shuffling papers, sorting them, then placing one in front of Sydney, "It's our Christmas party. Formal but not too formal, you know, festive." Her vision swept over Sydney's attire of day-old sweater and rumpled slacks. Her nose wrinkled with disapproval, "Dress, skirt, something like that, if you have one."

Sydney caught the hesitation and angled her narrowed vision to meet Cynthia who finished, "All the staff and authors get together. It starts at seven. Will we see you there?"

Subduing a frown, she knew she'd attend the party alone which certainly didn't set well with her. However duty called and she was newest on staff. If she didn't show, it would definitely be considered a hefty slap in the face to the higher-ups. She referenced her calendar to make a note, "Count me in. What time again? Seven?"

Cynthia nodded as her impeccably manicured hand made a note, "At the Atlanta Center. See you there. Remember, skirt or dress." She swiveled on one high heel and marched out.

Utterly annoyed, Sydney silently mimicked Cynthia then faced the window again, assuring herself the day would get better. It had to. Despite the fact this Melanie Griffith clone systematically bulldozed her attire was not going to trash her day, damn it. From the corner of her eye, Sydney saw her sway out and secretly prayed the goal post high heels might just snag in the carpet. Oh, the insecurities of some women. Sydney never felt obliged to jack her height to those proportions. Probably because she never enjoyed being laughed at. If Ms. Cynthia felt sexy walking with ballerina-erect feet, so be it.

"Witch." Sydney's hand raced to her mouth, surprised her thought found freedom. "Such a witch," the words repeated, making her realize Jason said it and not her. He'd approached her from behind, repeating the phrase. "You okay, honey? I don't see any blood. Don't let her bother you. You know, she wanted this job and was most displeased when you arrived."

"A promotion from public relations to assistant editor?" The concept blew her mind to even think about it. "How's that?"

Jason leaned in, his hand tucked quaintly at her hip, "You know the term 'casting couch'? She gives it a whole new meaning. I've heard she's quite limber."

Ah, the reason for the heels. Sydney finally understood and chuckled, sprouting the same reaction from Jason. "I'm sure there's something to be said for limber."

Rose's rather confused tone emerged from the intercom, "Uh, Sydney, you have a gift out here."

Both stared silently at the intercom, wondering why Rose didn't either continue or just bring the gift to the office. Sydney reacted first by pushing the talk button, "Be right there, Rose. Thank you."

Jason's lips pursed as he thought aloud, "Odd." He pressed the talk button himself, "Rose, how 'bout bringing that gift to Sydney?"

A moment passed, "Uh, this guy insisted she come get it herself."

Tiring of the verbal tennis match, Sydney asked, "Who is it?" *Probably Ethan*, she surmised. *It's another trick in his chaotic bag of pranks and I know it.*

"Dunno."

Sydney sighed, "Well, is he still there?"

"No."

Jason started to answer back but Sydney urged his hand away. He snorted in disapproval, "For pity's sake, this is nonsense. You're not at anyone's beck and call. I mean, don't you think this is odd?"

"Jason, most of what happens in my life is odd. Get used to it." She made her way to Rose's desk, seeing the flush in the young woman's cheeks. Sydney's stomach instinctively clenched. What had Ethan sent this time, more handcuffs? She waited guardedly like someone about to catch a time bomb. Instead, Rose bent down and, with a muted groan, heaved a vase of lavender roses onto the desk. A small sealed envelope hung from a stem. Sydney stepped closer, intrigued, completely enchanted. Sydney felt her hands shake slightly, "Who in the world would..." her voice trailed off.

With rounded eyes, Rose shook her head, "I dunno but unless he's got a police record, you'd be smart to keep him. He was bundled up like an Eskimo – part of the mystery, I'm sure."

"Nothing to do with the fact it's twenty-eight degrees out – I'm sure," Jason teased.

Rose threw him a warning glance, "He asked me to wait until he left then tell Sydney so I think he's being mysterious. He pinned a note to the stem and said, 'It's important she know how much I care but she shouldn't know who I am yet. You won't tell her what I look like, will you?' Well, I said no, of course."

Sydney leaned closer, "But you didn't mean it, of course. What did he look like, Rose?"

Briefly debating her quandary, Rose couldn't help but blurt, "He was *tall*," she indicated with her hands. By Sydney's account, he stood well over six feet. Rose continued, "Broad shoulders and he wore a Braves cap. He had black hair though. Thick, wavy black hair that you could run your fingers through. Oh, you could lose yourself in –"

"Rose," Jason deadpanned. "He's interested in Sydney."

Returning to reality, Rose bit, "I can dream, can't I?"

Sydney tried to place a face with the mystery. If not Ethan, who? Carefully, with trembling hands, she removed the note from its pink envelope that read "Dearest Sydney". Both Rose and Jason angled for a better view. Flipping the note open, Sydney saw masculine handwriting, its flair legible but stylish, "Angelo mio, mi manchi…" *My angel, I miss you.*

Jason flapped his hand, fanning himself, "He called you 'my angel'."

Sydney paused, "You know Italian?"

"Only the good parts. Read, honey. Our panties are in a bunch we're so anxious."

Sydney blushed hard. She knew this poem. She loved this poem and either someone stumbled into the fact or they already knew it. "It's called 'To' by Pushkin.

I remember the wonderful moment;

Before me you appeared,

Like a passing vision,

Like a spirit of pure beauty.

In the fatigue of mournful hopelessness,

In the unrest of a noisy restless world,
Echoed in me your tender voice
And your dear features in my dreams.

The years passed.
The rebellious gusts of the storm
Scattered the previous dreams,
And I forgot your tender voice,
Your heavenly features.

In the loneliness, in the gloom of exile
stretched quietly my days,
Without divinity, without inspiration,
Without tears, without life, without love.

My soul began to awaken:
And again you appeared,
Like a passing vision,
Like a spirit of pure beauty.

And my heart is beating in ecstasy,
And once more for it is born anew
Divinity, and inspiration,
And life, and tears, and love."

Sydney re-read the entire poem to ensure the words were actually there. Glancing at Jason and Rose, they both look genuinely wistful. Her brain accessed every file available for men she knew. Ethan hadn't delivered it. Had he sent someone to deliver it for him? Doubtful. Travis Shaw possessed no romantic bone in his diffident body so she nixed him as a candidate. He seemed rather relieved she left Savannah. And while Pushkin's works were renowned, Sydney hadn't seen this poem in print for several years. This person knew her preferences – they had to because she didn't buy into that destiny crap. The fairytale garbage ended the morning she laid eyes on Amanda and Ethan.

The phone rang, startling all three of them. The electronic ringer chirped twice more before Rose successfully palmed the receiver, "Fantasy Publishing, tenth floor. This is Rose, how may I help you?" A moment later she turned to Sydney, stammering, "Y-yes, j-just a moment, please." Eyes big as saucers, she covered the mouthpiece while proffering it to Sydney, "It's *him*."

Still stunned, her brow arched in question, "Ethan or..."

Jason leaned toward her whispering, "I think Rose means it's Pushkin man."

Now Sydney's eyes rounded much like Rose's. Jason's hand rested on her hip as a supportive gesture – and to urge her closer to the phone. She focused on the receiver as though it was a serpent waiting to strike. Reluctantly she took it, "Sydney Eatonton,"

"Do you like everything?" A deep, smooth voice awakened every sense and nerve in her body. A velvet tone, she noted, that stroked like a lover's touch. A perfect sex voice.

Sydney exhaled every word poised her tongue, probably because they were thoroughly inappropriate. This man was a stranger and she quite possibly could be the victim of a stalker. As though sensing her thoughts, he chuckled softly, somehow easing her worries. The sound also broke her trance, "Yes, the roses are beautiful and the poem – how did you know Pushkin is one of my favorites?"

"I exist to know and discover all your likes and desires. I want to bring you the delight your exquisite beauty brings to me."

Her cheeks flamed red hot. Both Jason and Rose's brows lifted to new heights. "Who is this?" Sydney asked, amazed that her tone softened to the same silky sound as his. She should probably be scared out of her mind but this man's affect on her totally reversed that instinct. The voice spoke again, caressing her with each word, "I am your admirer, of course."

"My admirer," she repeated quietly, nearly timidly. *My God, this is ridiculous. I'm reverting back to a teenager.*

"I'll be in touch again soon. Tesoro mio, ti penso sempre," the voice finished then the line went dead.

Sydney stared straight ahead, dumbfounded and unable to move, speak or squeak. She only thought about the man who owned that voice. That resonant sexy-as-hell, take-me-to-bed-this-instant voice. A shiver worked through her at the thought of his touch, how tender it would be. *He called me his treasure. His treasure…*

"Yoo-hoo, Sydney?" Jason called while leaning in to listen. He heard only silence then took the phone and hung up, "Do we get an update or do I need to notify a doctor? Because you look ready to faint."

"I… I am."

Rose rolled her computer chair behind Sydney and Jason eased her down by the shoulders, "Rose, we need a glass of water." He sank to one knee, "Did this man threaten you, honey?"

Finally, her vision lifted to his, "What? No, no, he didn't."

Rose returned with the water, "Did I miss anything?"

Jason frowned, "She's finally on the return trip home. Here, honey, have a drink."

Sydney grasped the glass with both shaking hands, "He didn't threaten me. He, well, he said he existed to know my likes and desires. When I asked who he was, he said an admirer and that he'd be in touch again soon and that he thought of me always. And he called me his treasure."

Jason melted onto her lap, all smiles and giggles, "Darling, where do you find these men and can you please give one to me?" He hugged her, "*Please?*"

Rose flung her hand across his shoulder, "Cut it out, ya dope. Sydney, did you recognize his voice?"

"Not one to-die-for syllable."

Logan refrained from doing a victory dance but he did grab another RC to celebrate. Somehow he always found a way to make her regress to that little girl in sixth grade. The pure bewilderment in her tone was priceless. He imagined her eyes were dinner plate size, those innocent, surprised green pools wondering what he might say next. More importantly what might *happen* next.

He knew one thing for sure. Sydney *was* intrigued and flattered because her voice reflected it. It took him most of the morning to find the lavender roses and finding twelve had been an absolute bitch. Women loved roses but Logan wanted something unusual for her. Something rare. Suddenly he began to feel better. Hearing her voice caused his hormones and hydraulics to surge but the wonder in her tone made it worthwhile.

Walking into Fantasy Publishing with the flowers had stirred enough interest he applauded himself for wearing the coat, glasses and hat. He'd parked in front of the twelve story mirrored building sporting the words "Fantasy Publishing" in bold purple script. The formally dressed doorman, an older man, swung the door open with a hushed comment, "Some young lady is lucky today."

Logan smiled, "Do you know Sydney Eatonton's floor?"

A glimmer of slyness twinkled in the elderly man's eyes, "Just so happens that I do. Tenth floor, Suite 12, sir." He added, "And good luck."

Normally, Logan would agree he needed it but he intended to hightail it out ASAP after delivery. He wanted to remain anonymous for a while. Enchant her, stroke her curiosity, let her feelings grow, if they would – then reveal his identity.

Entering the large foyer, Logan saw cover-work for novels mounted on the walls. Unfortunately, he only saw Sydney in them which made him harder than stone. He forced himself to stop fantasizing long enough to deliver the flowers. If he didn't, he'd teeter into her office with the biggest boner in history. He could only imagine it, "Hi,

Syd. Me and little Logan really missed you and we'd like to give you a proper welcome home. If you'll bend over your desk, we'll take over from there…"

As he passed by the board announcing all the employee's names and locations, he noticed Sydney's name had been added recently. "Senior Assistant Editor" it said. He was proud for her – the job obviously meant a lot to her and he was glad someone recognized her talent. To the right of her name followed her location, "Tenth floor, Suite 12" just like the doorman said. He hopped the first available elevator wishing it would move faster. The moment the doors slid back, Logan followed the softly lit hallway into the reception area. He rounded the corner and spied a vivacious redhead sitting behind a desk. She chattered constantly to someone on the phone until she saw the roses. All speaking ceased except a weak, "I gotta go," then she hung up. Logan had his speech rehearsed perfectly until the woman's open-mouth gape and wide eyes annihilated the whole of it. He could only hope Sydney reacted the same way.

Leaning across the desk, he whispered, "Is Sydney here?"

A mechanical nod answered him. Her vision never strayed from the arrangement. He hoisted the vase closer to her, "These are for her. Now, listen carefully, because it's important…" He scrapped together what he remembered of his instructions, asked if she understood then disappeared – before he charged into Sydney's office and bent her over her desk *then* said hello.

Logan grinned again. He'd rendered Sydney speechless with the flowers. And if she thought today was special, wait until tomorrow…

10

"It's an emergency," Ethan confided frantically. "I need to see you now." So to calm his brother, Logan agreed to meet him at Frisco's within the hour. Busy with morning rounds, Logan was surprised when his pager beeped. His brother rarely bothered him at work so he dropped everything to find a phone. Ethan sounded desperate; he needed to talk now, not that night, not tomorrow. Something was terribly wrong, he'd said, and his urgency spurred Logan to speed from the hospital all the way downtown, past the garish Fantasy building down to their favorite eatery. Before allowing him to sit, Ethan spilled his problem, "Sydney's seeing someone else."

"What?" Logan couldn't believe his ears. *This* was Ethan's emergency? That Sydney was dating? Tempering his anger and frustration, he ground through gnashed teeth, "Ethan, I just ran three red lights and committed several other traffic violations because I thought this was serious."

"It is. She's seeing someone else."

Resigned, Logan leaned back and exhaled loudly. Inevitably his baby brother managed to lose twenty years mentally when Sydney was around. Logan worried if Sydney suddenly married, Ethan might revert to sucking his thumb. Resolved to spend a few minutes talking shop about her, Logan promised himself no more than ten minutes then he'd return to work, "She's not allowed to?"

Ethan didn't answer. Logan pressed further, "You two aren't married so she can see other men. Are you seeing other women?"

"Only one. A dispatcher from DeKalb County and she ain't no Syd. Believe me on that."

Logan's anger built to new proportions. Ethan's arrogant attitude about women would eternally doom his brother, "And you expect Sydney to put her life on hold for you? She did once then caught you screwing Amanda. Don't ask her to pledge her life to you when you're still sowing wild oats, brother." If he wanted any chance with Sydney, he would have to stay true to her but then again, his brother wasn't Einstein. Still, he couldn't help himself, "Ethan, tell me. Are promotions at the department based on intelligence or longevity?"

Ethan waved the waitress over, answering, "What's that supposed to mean?"

Logan just shook his head. Their waitress approached with two coffees, "Morning Lieutenant. Morning Logan." Logan's name rolled low and sexy from her tongue and was followed with a wink and, "It's great to see you this morning."

Logan returned her wink with a smile, "And you as well, Brenda." The petite twenty-eight year-old blonde made her intentions quite clear every time he and Ethan ate at Frisco's. A friendly crush, he called it, though he realized with little encouragement, his nights would no longer be lonely or dull. True, she was attractive by society's standards and possessed a compassionate, pleasant personality. Logan enjoyed their flirting and verbal bantering. Brenda made brown-bagging his lunch every day a thing of the past. For nearly a year he entertained asking her out but held off for some reason. With Sydney's return, he realized why the date never materialized. He'd never felt so alive as he had since Syd came home to Atlanta.

Setting the cup down, Brenda tossed her long mane back to present Logan with her prettiest smile, "I fixed your coffee just as you like, cream with one sugar."

He did love her coffee. Brenda's coffee was paradise compared to his, which wavered between both extremes – something resembling either amber colored water or Vermont maple syrup. "Thank you, sweetheart. Did you pour my brother a decaf? He's having lady problems again and probably should remain calm, or as calm as he *can* be." Logan's statement hadn't sounded dire however Brenda, knowing Ethan only casually, received it as though the cup were filled with poison. Alarmed, her eyes widened and her hand darted forward to retrieve the mug. Ethan stopped her, "This is fine."

She shrugged then swiveled on one toe, her backside blatantly in Logan's sight. She tugged the hem of her pink skirt down and looked over her shoulder at him, "If you boys need anything, call me."

Both brothers watched her sway back to the counter, Logan with quiet admiration, Ethan with a predatory smile, "She's got the hots for you, you know. Why don't you take her out?"

Logan sipped the coffee and exhaled, contented with thoughts of

Sydney and the smooth, richness coating his palate, "Because I've set my sights on a different woman."

"Really? Who?"

Having no interest in sharing that aspect of his life, he shook his head, "How do you know Syd's seeing someone?"

Ethan explained he dropped by the day before to discover a vase of lavender roses on her desk along with a note she greedily snatched up before he could. After some encouragement – Logan reckoned it was more like goading – she finally displayed the note. Rather haughtily, Ethan added. Logan had no clue his brother knew the word, much less what it meant. Ethan surmised she threw the note in his face because she wanted him to be jealous, "I told her to stop seeing the clown."

Logan concealed his amazement of her openness. He assumed she'd keep the admirer under wraps *because* of Ethan's persistent jealousy, "And she said…"

Ethan's tone dropped to a grumble, "She told me to shove it and get out. She'd see whoever she wanted."

Logan could tell it hurt his brother to repeat it but Sydney was right. He should shove the idea, "La belle dame sans merci." *The beautiful lady without mercy.* At least according to Ethan.

Ethan shot him a fiery glare, "Don't. The foreign thing is wearing thin with me."

Logan played ignorant, "Foreign thing?"

"The bastard is writing to her in Italian. Schmaltzy crap like 'my angel.'"

"Bastard indeed," Logan smiled behind the coffee cup. "Women despise that kind of thing." He sat the empty cup down and waved at Brenda for a refill. As if anticipating his request, she cheerfully sidled up to him with a carafe, "I'm honored, Dr. Calhoun. Two cups today."

Ethan interrupted his brother's reply with, "Brenda, tell me something." He reached for her hand, held it softly, "A handsome guy walks up to you, takes your hand and starts speaking Italian. What do you do?"

"Oh, Lieutenant," she blushed, clearly smitten with the question, "I do believe I'd swoon. Go ahead, say something to me."

Logan propped his arm across the back of the booth, smirking, "Yes, Lieutenant. Make the lady swoon."

Ethan kissed her hand, "C'è l'hai un bel culo."

As Logan sipped his coffee, he carefully swallowed before choking on shock. First indignation then disgust crossed Brenda's features as she jerked her hand back. Ethan, on the other hand, grinned. Studying the others, however, it dawned that he'd utterly screwed up somehow.

Brenda gripped the carafe rigidly, Logan noticed, and before she dumped hot coffee in Ethan's lap, he diffused the situation, "Brenda, you'll have to excuse my baby brother. He's, well, he's just learning Italian."

Ethan's eyes rounded, "What'd I say?"

"What had you intended to say?" His brother inquired calmly.

"'You have such a sweet touch.'"

The anger slowly melted from Brenda's expression but she kept a cautious eye on Ethan while ambling back to the counter. Logan explained, "Well, you said, 'You have such a sweet *tush*.'"

"Oh, God." Ethan's head fell into his hands, his voice booming loud enough for most everyone to hear, "Sorry, Brenda."

Logan leaned closer, "Do that with Syd and you'll go home with bruises and walk funny for a week."

Ethan stirred his coffee, "Then tell me what to do. I'm desperate. I don't want to lose her again."

"Let her see this guy and don't pester her about it."

The spoon clattered to the table, his temper festering, "Aren't you supposed to support me in my days of crisis? Where's the brotherly advice?"

Deciding he'd had enough, Logan gathered his coat, "That is my brotherly advice – let her go. You screwed up when you slept with Amanda. You pay since you dragged me from work for this." As he passed Brenda, he blew a kiss to her, "Come sei bella." *How beautiful you are.* A girlish grin livened her pretty face and she blew a kiss back, thanking him.

11

Sydney arrived to work early. Stepping off the elevator, she heard the prattle of voices 'oohing' and 'ahhing'. Instantly her stomach twisted. The noise came from the vicinity of her office. She wheeled, hoping to catch the elevator before the doors closed. "Run away, run away!" The Monty Python catch phrase seemed the perfect solution to this problem. Unfortunately, she bumped smack into the gold sliding doors and she stood staring at her reflection. She truly looked as miserable as she felt.

She took a deep breath to calm herself down then resigned herself to face the music. Coming to work evolved into a chaotic circus and she felt like an acrobat without a net. She passed Rose who smiled sweetly – now the situation set her teeth on edge. Something was wrong and with her luck Ethan was the culprit. Since he saw the admirer's roses and read his note, she wouldn't put anything past Ethan now, "Is it even safe to enter my office?"

"Of course, sweetie. You're not in any danger."

"That's a matter of opinion." Cautiously rounding the corner to her office, the sight of ten people huddled around the doorway made her backpedal into Rose. She didn't want to see this, experience this or deal with this – whatever *this* was. But Jason already caught sight of her and blocked her escape, "For the record, I have no idea."

"At least you admit it. Why are you blocking my office?"

He timidly grinned, "Because I've seen how you react to surprises." He glanced in, "Yes, everything's ready. Your chair, the glass of water..."

Sydney frowned while guiding him out of the way. She'd cope with Ethan's jealousy head-on, she vowed. But when she stepped in the office, her legs liquefied. Then her eyes bugged. She was sure her heart stopped if only briefly.

Jason braced her shoulders, giddy with joy, "Aren't they simply marvelous?"

They were but there were *so many* of them. Red and yellow roses covered her desk from stem to stern. All positioned with their flowers facing the door, they alternated red and yellow into a giant fan shape across her desk. There wasn't one layer or even two. There were three layers of gloriously fragrant beautiful roses lining her desk. "Oh my..." she breathed, the surreal scene stealing every coherent word from her brain.

Jason whispered, "Isn't he fabulous, honey? I tremble to think about tomorrow."

So did she, quite frankly. Whoever this admirer was, he wanted to impress her. What he didn't realize was, she passed impressed thirty roses ago. Now she sat squarely in the middle of stunned.

She willed her legs toward the desk to find a note sitting atop the arrangement, along with two books. She had to sit down for this but she wanted to do it without an audience. Asking everyone to return to work, she watched the begrudging group disperse as she unfolded the note. The same masculine, legible handwriting greeted her, "Dearest Sydney, each petal represents one reason you are special to me. You will discover I never end my quest for your heart. Your Devoted Admirer."

Why did her insides coil warmth from her ears to her toes? It should have scared the living wits out of her. No one except Ethan knew where she worked. The writing wasn't Ethan's, grief, the *words* weren't Ethan's. He was sweet but he wasn't sensual.

The books, one a compilation of works by Dante, Rosetti and Petrarch, the other of Pushkin, Brodsky and Akhmatova, thoroughly intrigued her. Only a handful of people – mostly family – knew these were her favorite poets. She noticed a red satin ribbon bookmark in one poetry book. She opened it to a poem by Petrarch called "Bound To Love", another poem she knew well. Silently she read it:

> Oh blessed be the day, the month, the year,
> the season and the time, the hour, the instant,
> the gracious countryside, the place where I was
> struck by those two lovely eyes that bound me;

> and blessed be the first sweet agony
> I felt when I found myself bound to Love,
> the bow and all the arrows that have pierced me,
> the wounds that reach the bottom of my heart.

> And blessed be all of the poetry

I scattered, calling out my lady's name,
and all the sighs, and tears, and the desire;

blessed be all the paper upon which
I earn her fame, and every thought of mine,
only of her, and shared with no one else.

Was it possible to fall in love with a stranger? Sydney supposed so because she swore she was. This man knew what she liked. He seemed to know *her*.

Jason spoke first, "Get a drink of water, honey. You've got that look again."

She did. Then, as if on cue, the phone rang. Sydney held Rose off to answer it herself, "Sydney Eatonton,"

"Ah, lovely Sydney. Was today's gift satisfactory?" It was *the* voice. And it caressed her with her own name. Threads of fire spiraled down through her breasts all the way to her toes. A noticeable shiver worked through her, making Jason and Rose lean closer to the conversation.

She stared at the enormous fan of velvet roses spanning her desk, still in shock. Dozens of beautiful flowers surrounded her, topped with a mysterious note and two books of her favorite poets. Hushed words stammered past her lips, "Satisfactory? That's a first degree understatement. You did this yourself?"

"Of course, sweetheart." The voice deepened to a gentle rumble, "I hope you don't mind – I promise I didn't touch anything except a few papers. Those can be found on the cabinet behind you."

Sydney swiveled. Sure enough, the papers remained stacked as she'd left them, only moved so the flowers didn't damage them. "I see them. Thank you for all these beautiful gifts. It would be nice to thank you by name. I mean, I'm speechless that anyone would care so much."

"You are my soul, the very beat of my heart. The moment I saw you again, the flame of hope and love burned brighter inside me."

His voice and words generated a heat inside her she hadn't felt for years. Whoever he was, he knew how to arouse her. If she only knew his identity...

As though reading her mind, he assured, "You'll eventually recognize who I am. I must go now but I'll leave you with this thought. Cara mia, ti voglio bene."

Sydney's brain raced to remember her Italian. Lord, after sixteen years, those four brief years of high school Italian courses were decidedly rusty. Cara mia – my darling. Ti voglio bene – I love you. "I love you," she whispered without thinking. He said he loved her. *Oh... My... God...*

"I do, Sydney. I love you." He murmured again then quickly hung up.

She stood speechless, her vision fixed on the note in front of her. Mesmerized by the whispered declaration, her body rejected any effort to react. To even simply move. She merely swallowed.

Worried, Jason positioned himself on one knee at her feet, staring eagerly up, "Honey," he snapped his fingers, "you told him you loved him. Did you mean to?"

She didn't hear him. Instead her mind re-ran the conversation. "You'll eventually recognize who I am." *I know him. Or knew him at one time.*

Jason's hands framed her face, trying to draw her attention, "You're scaring us again."

His touch broke the spell and their vision met, "Jason, this is weird."

"Darling, it's good of you to finally notice." He handed her the water glass, "Now, why did you declare your love for this stranger?"

"He's not a stranger. He said I would 'recognize' who he was. Like I knew him."

He dropped his head on her knee, "Thank heavens. I was beginning to think we needed Ethan to investigate."

Like a slap in the face, Ethan's name sobered her. She gently took Jason by the earring and lifted him to face her, "We're not telling Ethan anything else. He's not my lord and master."

His cheeks flushed with color as she held on, he replied, "Sounds like someone wants to be. Speaking of Ethan, have you decided what you're wearing to the Christmas party?"

Now she released him, replying cautiously, "Why? Jason, I *do* have dresses and I do own skirts, contrary to what Ms. Andrews thinks."

"Forget her. I was thinking you want to look extra spectacular in case Pushkin was there." He flashed a sinister grin.

"He'll be there like Ethan will be. No need to impress someone who isn't attending."

"Honey, Ethan will be there. He and other off-duty officers have been hired as security."

The revelation stunned her into silence. Her mouth worked with no sound emerging except, "Wha?"

He took her arm, "Now, don't panic your pretty noggin. If you trust me to help, I'll make sure you are the hit of the show."

Where *had* her voice gone? The party would be stressful enough but for Ethan to be there as well... God, it was too much. With her luck, Pushkin *would* be there. "Jason, thank you but you hardly know me."

He stepped in front of her and with crossed arms, he contemplated while giving her a visual going over. She watched him circle her, and sensed him taking mental notes. "Why do I feel like an experiment?" she asked.

Concentration knitted his brow and he tapped his index finger softly against his lips, "Red. Definitely, red. Leather too. You'd look so hot, honey. Pushkin couldn't keep his hands off you."

"Leather?" The mere mention shocked her back to reality and into retreat mode mentally *and* physically, "Jason, no. I've never worn it or wanted to."

A crafty smirk curled his mouth, "Then it's time you started. You've got no clue what you have. You're perfect for leather." He reached forward and barely stroked the curves of her breasts, "These will need more exposure. They will drive Pushkin wild so we need just the right thing to push him over the edge. If he's there, of course."

Sydney straightened her shoulders while wearing off the sensation of his touch and thoughts of her admirer, "Listen, it's a party, a *company* party. I can't dress in leather."

Jason, fluttering about in a frantic but focused manner, put his notes to paper, "Trust me, honey. When it comes to these parties, Atlanta is a different universe compared to Savannah. Here, we live up to the Fantasy name. There, they remind me of IBM." He glanced up from his writing and smiled into her bewildered features, "Do you mind if I take thirty minutes off? I promise, it will be very beneficial."

She waved him off, "Go ahead. But if you make me look like a sideshow in the French Quarter, I'll kill you. I'd rather go as Lady Godiva."

"Hmm… *That's* an idea. Certainly would get everyone's attention. Even mine. See ya later, honey." He trotted out, gleeful as a child with a new toy.

Sydney rushed after him, "And no leather either!" The impact of her outburst hit her and as heads turned in her direction, she cowered back into her office. She flopped in her chair, realizing she'd be grateful to survive Christmas unscathed in some manner. The phone rang, thankfully taking her mind from the past few minutes. She prayed it was Pushkin again, "Sydney Eatonton,"

"Hello, sugar." Ethan sounded most pleased at her tone. "Mind if I come over and play?"

It took a massive effort to calm her racing heart. The fierce banging made her slightly faint so she grasped the desk for stability and prayed her voice didn't reflect her disappointment, "Ethan, I'm really busy."

"Sure. Just wanted to tell you I'm looking forward to the party."

Rubbing her temple and willing the growing pang away, she replied, "Yeah, I just found out you'd be there."

"I thought we could go as a couple. I'll pick you up –"

"That's sweet but no. Your job is security and mine is to mingle. Sorry."

"We'll make it work. Listen, I've heard some stories about the guys working at Fantasy and they're not good. I want people to know you and I are together so they don't get any ideas."

"Listen to *me*, Ethan. My job that night is to be available and congenial. I cannot be either if you're on my heels like some..." She gnashed her teeth, trying to control her temper while trying to conjure the right word. She gave up and settled for, "Like some little poodle. Don't pressure me."

"It's not pressure, Syd, and I prefer to think of myself as a protective Great Dane."

Sydney blew out a breath. She heard his voice harden slightly, "It's taking care of you, I want to do it and you're gonna let me, damn it. God, woman, you were *never* this stubborn –"

"I gotta go and do not continue to entertain this silly plan. It won't work. Goodbye, Ethan." She placed the phone down and asked Rose to hold all calls from him. Rubbing her temples harder, she purposefully evicted the conversation from her mind. Too bad she couldn't do the same with the headache. Reaching in her desk, she retrieved two aspirin. She'd be lucky if she wasn't fired before Friday, which would consequently save her from wearing whatever Jason was buying for her. Good God, how had her life gotten so screwed up?

The last thing she needed was Officer Ethan hanging on her like a dictatorial lover. Insistent or not, she wouldn't allow it. Who did he think he was anyway? She could take care of herself. She lived alone in Savannah and lived alone now. She hadn't required a man's help for anything except heavy lifting, electrical work and a tune up on the Camaro.

The longer Sydney thought about Ethan, the angrier she got. Afraid she'd flirt? Afraid she might be flattered by another man's advances? *That* was it. He feared Pushkin would be there and he'd have to endure seeing her with another man. Well too bad...

Almost immediately the door opened again. Still seething over Ethan's Neanderthal behavior, she swiveled in the chair, still wielding the sour expression.

Her features instantly immobilized Jason. He obviously didn't know whether to run or hide. He saw the hateful glare melt from her and he sat the shopping bags in the chair by the door, "Honey, you look... unhappy. What's wrong?"

Ignoring his concern, she bounced to her feet, determined more than ever to kick Ethan Calhoun's backside, "What did you find?"

He grinned, winked and withdrew one of the purchases, "Leather!"

Still boiling in the anger Ethan provoked, she stared at the minuscule black leather skirt vowing, "I'll wear it. What else is there?"

He giggled with joy, "Darling, it was the most fabulous trip. I kept thinking 'how does Sydney want to come across?' Then I went with my gut instinct. It's sort of 'dominatrix meets girl next door.'"

She leaned against the wall and crossed her arms, "Ditch the girl next door. She needs a life."

"Oh, *honey*! You make life worth living! I was *so hoping*..." His hands quivered with excitement as he retrieved a fire engine red silk blouse, "Am I good or what?"

She nodded with approval, "Shoes, Jason. What about those?"

He realized her seriousness but still basked in his success, "Red spike heels, darling. Higher than a hippie on LSD. And with your natural height, oh, Lord A'mighty..." He emphasized while digging for more, "I hope you didn't mind but I took the liberty of undergarments as well."

"It's fine. What did you get?"

"What dominatrix doesn't like the feel of lace once in a while? Here's a little ditty for a bra."

Little ditty was right. There was barely anything to it. The flimsy black number was intended to hold but not totally conceal the breasts. The more she looked at it, the more sinful she felt. Dangling it on her pinkie finger, she weighed it, "This is going to hold these?" She pointed to her breasts.

"You'd be surprised. Let's see. Oh, and a nice garter with stockings, of course."

"Where are the panties?"

Jason blushed up past his ears. Sydney knew she was in trouble. He cleared his throat, "Oh, you wanted panties too. Um, well..."

"Jason, I can't go to a company party," her voice lowered, "without panties. I know this isn't IBM but it's no Slut Central either."

"I love you, honey. You're so dramatic." His hand flicked a minuscule slice of fabric from the bag and dangled it before her, "I picked up a v-string so you can feel the leather skirt against your skin. It'll make you feel so sexy, not to mention how you'll look. Even if Pushkin isn't there, you'll drive Ethan wild with the first look."

"I want to do more than that. I want to bring him to his knees with jealousy. That'll show him his name is *not* tattooed on my rear."

12

"I love you." The whispered words elated Logan, giving him renewed hope. She'd parroted them with astonishment, as though it was the first time she'd heard them. He knew Ethan said them habitually but his brother loved in a totally different sense, a possessive one. Logan loved in a more cherishing way. His only problem now was to overcome what he called The Logan Effect. Some men were afflicted with commitment angst, he was afflicted with commitment passion. For one woman who disliked him – or didn't like him enough to marry him. If she knew her admirer was Logan Calhoun, he stood a good chance she'd reject him again. He just needed to continue taking his steps carefully.

"Dr. Calhoun, are you okay?"

Logan turned to face the young brunette sitting on the exam table – a brunette that strongly resembled Ms. Eatonton at age eighteen. A spark of awareness flickering in her eyes made him edgy, like she read his thoughts. He smiled, trying to ease her concern and his stomach, "I'm fine, Amy. Just let me check that knee and with any luck you can return to the basketball team next week."

"Good," she grinned. "Mrs. Turner hoped I'd be ready for the playoffs."

That smile… If Logan hadn't met Amy's mother, he'd have sworn Sydney was responsible for the mirror image sitting in front of him. Her dark hair flowed softly past her shoulders, her figure trim and curvy, her smile devastating.

Logan busied himself gently probing the girl's knee. The incision healed quickly considering the work he'd done. The way she swung her legs when he entered told him this girl followed his instructions to the letter and mended in record time – and being the star player, she forewarned him she *would* be ready for the playoffs one way or another. *Sydney played basketball and ran track in high school*, his mind taunted. *The girl ran like the wind.*

"I think you've got a girl on your mind. What's her name?"

Out of the mouths of babes, he thought. Was he blushing? The temperature in the room escalated to roasting. He sighed and unbuttoned his collar for room and air, hoping to relieve some of the discomfort.

Before he denied her assumption, Amy leaned closer, nudging his arm, "C'mon, Dr. Calhoun. You owe me that. After all, I let you operate on my knee when I could have opted for Dr. Chaney."

"You don't like Dr. Chaney and I know it." He tested the range of her leg, "Plus, you said I was cute."

"You are and I don't like to see you sad. Who is she?"

Instinctive, he thought. Women possessed incredible intuitive skills. She wanted to know then okay, "An old love from high school. She recently moved back to Atlanta. Her name is Sydney." He tenderly pressed around the incision area, "Does that hurt?"

She shook her head, "So what's the problem?"

"The age old dilemma called unrequited love."

Amy's green eyes darkened, "Did she come back and, you know…"

"Rebuff me?" Logan chuckled, "No. It was sixteen years ago but I am trying to woo her again. Hopefully I'll have better luck this time."

"Ah," she said, then nibbled her bottom lip nervously, trying to build her courage, "So is it working? Because if it doesn't, I'm free for the wooing."

For some reason he and Amy connected as friends the day she hobbled into the emergency room after trashing her knee during basketball practice. Admittedly, he probably treated her more personably than most patients because she resembled Sydney. Amy hadn't exactly shied from his attention either. Over the following weeks, they became totally relaxed with each other – no doubt the easiness was the reason for her forward nature today. His smile relaxed and he patted her knee, "I hope it's working and I do appreciate the offer but you're eighteen –"

"Ditch the age excuse, Doc. It's not like I'm in diapers, you know. I mean, what does she look like anyway? Is she a brunette, a blonde?" Then teased, "Or are redheads more your style?"

Noticing she visually skimmed his attire, a green oxford shirt and tan khakis, he decided to briefly halt the exam. An eighteen year-old and a thirty-six year-old. A flattering image however he had a feeling Mr. and Mrs. Hughes might disagree, as well as the hospital board, the Georgia Board of Medicine and other powerful institutions that dearly loved to castrate physicians for inappropriate conduct. Logan pondered an explanation, "Amy, you look amazingly like her. Right down to that impish gleam in your eyes. Let me see how this goes with her first."

She conceded with a shrug, "Keep my number though."

"Will do, hon." He made a note on her chart, stating, "Looks like you're ready to go next week. I'll give you a reinstatement. Don't get your knee in a jam or your next date with me will be on an operating table." While he was turned, he heard her hop down and pull the sweats over her hips. He let a few moments pass before facing her, handing her the note. This time she spoke, "Thanks. And good luck with Sydney." Amy exited the room, waving goodbye. Logan waved back, whispering, "I'll need it."

He scrawled a few more notes on her chart, looked it over then noticed he hadn't given her a follow up appointment. Quickly, he scribbled one out and rushed after her. Down two hallways and around three corners into a large reception area, he spied her near the door, "Amy!"

The girl turned with a lifted brow and knowing grin, "Change your mind already?"

His breathing heavy from running, her playful reference split his face in a grin, "I'll see you in a month, hon. Same time, same room. Is it a date?"

She plucked the appointment card from his hand, winking, "It's a date."

Logan struggled to catch his breath. That girl would be his undoing unless Sydney got there first. Her backside swayed out the door, a nice scene for Logan since he'd only seen her limping from her injuries and surgery.

A laugh near him broke his concentration. That voice. He recognized that voice. Gradually he turned to see the source. Upon seeing her, his heart leaped into his throat, the roar of blood in his ears nearly drowned out all noises except her beautiful voice. Sydney. As Amy exited, Sydney and another woman entered and sat a few rows away, facing him.

He eased into the nearest chair. His legs threatened to give way with the sight. She wore a blue skirt and white silk blouse that just invited him to unwrap her like a perfectly decorated present. And those lofty heels merely inspired him to fantasize further.

Sydney hadn't changed except to grow sexier if that was possible. Her face looked as beautiful as he'd remembered. Minimal makeup and no blemishes. And the radiance of her smile brought him to his knees. Her petite build, slim waist and long legs hadn't changed, only gotten lovelier over time. Sydney's long, wavy hair remained as thick and luscious as in high school.

The redhead sitting with her spoke just loud enough he overheard, "Then his brother called?"

Sydney blushed. He'd forgotten how gorgeously she blushed. "Yes," she said lowly, "and Ethan let him assume we were busy, you know, doing something."

"And you weren't?" The redhead appeared confused. Or was it disappointed?

"No, Rose, we weren't. I had my clothes on. I tried to yell the fact Ethan handcuffed us together against my will then lost the key but Ethan covered my mouth. We were locked together all night like that."

Logan wanted to laugh. Leave it to Ethan to always screw up with Sydney.

Rose asked the one question he wanted to, "So how did you get loose?"

"Ethan's partner had to unlock us. Needless to say, Mr. Calhoun is slightly embarrassed over that."

Logan stood and meandered his way behind them. Positioning himself directly behind Sydney, he leaned back, inhaling her scent mixed with a light flowery perfume. He stopped himself from groaning. For the first time in sixteen long years, he sat within touching distance of this beautiful creature. Curls of her long hair draped over the back of her chair, begging his fingers to explore them. Rose whispered something that caused Sydney to turn suddenly, the consequent motion swept her hair across the back of his neck. Logan couldn't stop this groan. Evidently the sound emanated louder than he realized and Sydney turned, glanced at the back of his head. He purposefully remained motionless or else he'd explode with desire. He'd forget the admirer angle and draw her into a soul-reaching kiss.

A delicate touch on his shoulder brought him back to the moment. It had to be Sydney. Her sultry voice doomed him wholly, even as she offered an apology.

His silence unnerved the two women and he reached for her hand. The instant he brushed her fingers, they both startled slightly, "No problem," he answered in his deep tone. Had her hand lingered a second longer, Logan knew he'd have been destined for a day long case of blue balls.

Rose bowed back in her seat to see his face. Logan heard her whisper, "He's cute." He reached for an issue of Men's Health magazine as he felt Sydney turn also. Rose propped her elbow on the seat's back, staring like a teenager. She leaned closer to Sydney, "Maybe he's Pushkin."

Pushkin? What the hell was she saying? Sydney studied him a moment longer, "I wouldn't be that lucky, Rose. Admirers aren't always Cary Grant gorgeous."

Ah, her admirer. So his nickname was Pushkin, was it? Now, for some reason, he wanted her to know, to realize, to recognize it was him. Impatience reigned over common sense. Enchanted by her nearness and intoxicating scent, he leaned back to whisper something. Rose, the redhead, spoke instead, "You know, he *does* favor Pushkin. Mmm, that hair... Hair like that gives you an itch you want to spend a lifetime scratching."

"Down, girl," her friend advised. "You're here for an MRI, not a shot of epinephrine. Keep thinking about it and you'll get a rash."

Logan chuckled despite himself. Sydney joined him, "See? Even he agrees."

Rose didn't laugh, "I'm serious. He looks kinda like him."
He heard Sydney's breath catch. She'd taken Rose's comment to heart which meant recognition might be imminent. He sensed her lingering closer as though trying to see his face without appearing obvious. Then she inquired, "Pardon me, but do you know anything about Alexander

Pushkin?"

Logan closed the magazine, knowing the situation spun wildly out of control. It was up to him to stop the ride, "Pushkin the poet? No, 'fraid I don't know much at all." He stood, took one step forward then stopped. For some reason, he could stop his feet from moving but not his mouth – the one part of him that damned him every time, "Only that he published his first poem at fifteen and graduated from the Imperial Lyceum. 'I Loved You Once' is one of my favorite poems." Then he began the trek back to his office. Quickly because the redhead registered recognition. Sydney would follow, catch him and he'd have ruined his only chance with her.

Sydney sat mystified, the poem gently flowing in her mind like a warm tide.

> I loved you once, nor can this heart be quiet;
> For it would seem that love still lingers there;
> But do not you be further troubled by it;
> I would in no wise hurt you, oh, my dear;
> I loved you without hope, a mute offender;
> What jealous pangs, what shy despairs I knew!
> A love as deep as this, as true, as tender...

A tugging at her sleeve brought her from the poignant verse. Rose continued the campaign of subtle yanking while Sydney thought

through the last few moments. Had she just met her admirer in person?
The voice could have been his, hard to be totally sure. But the
information about Pushkin – *that* just seemed too coincidental.
Evidently, Rose agreed because she finally smacked Sydney's shoulder,
"It's *him*. It's Pushkin. Wake up and go catch him!"

She launched upward from her chair, the spell broken. Seeing
him turn a corner up ahead, she started running to keep him in her sights
but as quickly as he appeared, he was gone. Near tears, she realized Rose
was right. He *was* her admirer and thanks to her hesitancy, he'd slipped
right through her fingers. All the twists and turns in the hallways
confused her and now she couldn't find her way to him or back to the
waiting room. He, however navigated the floor with such ease it
astounded her. Did he work here in some capacity? Was he a doctor?
He hadn't worn a doctor's coat. Instead his handsome form fit perfectly
in the oxford and khakis like a magazine model. He was irresistibly
attractive, at least from the backside. Tall and muscular with black, wavy
hair cut short enough to run her fingers through. You could lose yourself
in it… For some reason, Sydney felt a sudden itch developing – just like
Rose said…

13

Friday evening. Sydney eagerly anticipated the event to meet other employees and the authors of Fantasy's books. Mostly she wanted to make Ethan Calhoun sweat. Sydney parked her car which seemed half a mile away and sashayed to the entrance of the Atlanta Center. The company Christmas party exploded into a massive gathering of people she hadn't expected. Maybe two hundred, she thought. But between trying to park the car among the hundreds of others and the hike to the front door, she re-evaluated the situation. There were probably four hundred people in attendance.

Years of wearing high heels accustomed her to walking on surfaces such as the parking lot's choppy asphalt. But these shoes, the shoes from Hell, nearly tripped her half a dozen times in her apartment before she gained solid footing. Sydney took great care while making her way to the front door of the auditorium. The heels augmented her height to 5'10", nearly 5'11". It was like standing on the Empire State Building but the longer she wore them, the sexier she felt. Not to mention how the leather skirt embraced her thighs and bottom and the silk of the blouse and lace bra caressed her skin like a lover's touch.

Initially, she feared spilling out of the bra but then after wearing it a while, she realized they accentuated but still safely held her. Jason's talent for dolling women up could easily be a side business for him.

Sydney looked dressed to kill – at least that's what two guys from the fourth floor said as they wolf-whistled their admiration. They barked their approval, thinking she was an author attending the party. When they discovered she was a senior assistant editor, they backed down with numerous apologies, slinking off like whipped puppies.

After what seemed thirty minutes, she reached the door and recognized Ethan's partner John who checked the ID's of the attendees, "Hey John," she greeted.

He turned and his choked voice told her the outfit was a total success. She now stood eye level with the burly cop who practically blushed as his blue eyes swept her from top to bottom, "Wow, you look…" he stammered for the correct word. She waited patiently with a pleasant smile and he finally blurted, "Outstanding."

Mission accomplished, she beamed secretly. "Thank you, John. You're joining the party, aren't you?"

His hands went in his trouser pockets. "Uh," hoarseness now appeared in his voice, "I have to work the door but I'll join you later…"

Sydney winked, "See you inside." She stepped in, hearing him clear his throat then grab his handy-talkie, "Calhoun, Sydney just arrived and Godalmighty, wait till you see her…"

A satisfied smile adorned her lips. She breezed into the large reception room filled with people. Overrun with them, in fact. Hundreds upon hundreds milled about in dresses, skirts or suits. Some dressed somewhat similar to her outfit but she prided herself on how sexy she looked – or felt, at least.

On the far wall a neon sign flickered "Fantasy" in its trademark purple script. The room, separated into two areas, a dining and dance area, abounded with purple and pink accents from tablecloths to the tortes lining the dessert table. She hadn't wanted to eat from the buffet – frankly her stomach couldn't handle the load gracefully. Even looking at the prime rib or garlic chicken flip-flopped her stomach. A healthy shot of Mylanta at a quiet corner table sounded best.

The thought of meeting *everyone* at Fantasy Publishing intimidated her but *seeing* them in one room, staff and authors all, materialized the daunting fact. Fantasy was a huge business and being a senior assistant editor meant she wielded a mighty power. Not as mighty as George Kelso, the president, or Becky Collins, the senior editor. Her position was more third in the pecking order. Perusing the auditorium, Sydney couldn't locate either so she meandered toward people she knew from the ninth and tenth floors. A waiter dressed like a Chippendale dancer offered her a glass of champagne from a silver serving tray. Kindly refusing, she found herself blushing when he pouted a plea and handed her a glass anyway, "Come on, beautiful. For me, please."

Nodding with a polite thank you, she sipped from the fluted crystal glass. This experience proved to be a one-eighty from the Savannah office party. She'd graduated from paper cups to crystal and from a portable radio to a full range sound system that could make a person's ears bleed. Everything literally overwhelmed her.

Decadence thrived here with half-dressed, over-sexed waiters and waitresses and costumed servers at the serving line and dessert table. A couple dressed as Caesar and Cleopatra served desserts while a provocative Mr. and Mrs. Claus made sure guests had drinks. As the latter pair breezed past dressed in Santa hats, red g-strings and strategically placed fur tufts and jingle bells, Sydney forced herself to slowly absorb the scene.

She scanned the room again. When she saw Ethan, both dread and relief washed over her. He dressed semi-casually in an olive green pullover and khaki slacks with his shield clipped to his belt. Not bad for a man who lived in jeans the whole time she'd known him. Ethan appeared extremely anxious himself – looking for her. Tipping his chin up, he scoured the crowd. She shook hands with a few people, introduced herself, all while mingling closer until he saw her. She knew the instant he did. She felt his brown eyes warm her, nearly taking her breath away.

Ethan's jaw plummeted to his chest. "Syd?" he whispered to himself. Good God, what had she done to herself? What had she done to him? His gut tightened when the cleavage, the *amount* of cleavage, graced his eager vision. Her breasts obviously wanted to attend the party au natural, or basically so. Her dark waves kissed the tops of her breasts, a few stray tendrils caressed around the prominent nipples poking against the blouse. That red silk number might as well have been a red flag she waved at Ethan. "Come and get me, if you think you're man enough," it goaded.

Obviously a few men did. Several approached her, put their arms around her, hugged her or kissed her. Some did all three. Ethan grunted. "She's mine, she's mine, she's mine," he chanted under his breath. Upon separating from a man's embrace, she caught Ethan's eye and winked.

"Here Comes Santa Claus" began in the background and he realized Santa may not be the only one coming tonight. Oh God, his erection hurt. After he got a load of those legs, it hurt to the point of exploding. Black hosiery delicately cloaked long, muscular legs. They reminded him of Rockette legs. Legs he remembered by heart so well, he recalled kissing her behind the knees drove her wild. Legs that ended on red spike heels, the points tapering to the width of ice picks. She did this on purpose, he seethed. Torturing him so utterly. She *never* dressed like this. Never in her life. Did she? He hadn't actually known her for sixteen long years. Maybe this was the other side of Sydney. A wilder side developed while living in Savannah. She certainly seemed comfortable in the getup. And she exuded sexuality out the ears, something she appeared to realize and use to her benefit.

Another man, this one in his early forties, slid his arm around her waist and she smiled at him. The returning smile indicated he felt very comfortable touching her. Ethan instantly wanted to kill him, whoever he was. She'd been in Atlanta a short time – too short to know this creep that well. He squinted with disapproval as he propelled himself toward her. Seeing him pound his way to her, he noticed her apprehensive expression. Then it settled into a cocky, self-assured grin as she eased into the man's embrace, a move that reinforced Ethan's purpose – to remove the offending touch and talk sense into Sydney. Upon approaching her, the group she spoke with halted their conversation evidently because of his glare.

"Something wrong, Lieutenant?" She inquired with the same seductive tone.

He stood a moment, his body begging him to intimately explore this beautiful creature standing in front of him. To visually sate himself then start exploring with his tongue. Swallowing the urge, he replied, "I need a word with you, *Ms. Eatonton.*" The sharp emphasis on her name indicated his degree of frustration. Her brow lifted incredulously but he gave her no time to verbalize a rejection. He excused them and ushered her to a remote corner. Sydney's expression darkened, "That was rude, Ethan. That was my boss, you know, the *president* of Fantasy Publishing?"

"You mean the lecher with his hand on your ass?" The venom stung hot and furious with each syllable.

Sydney appeared genuinely shocked. Ethan's protective effort seemed to surprise her. Sure, she'd call it outright jealousy but he knew the truth. Sometimes a man just had to act on impulse to get a woman's attention. With Sydney's degree of independence, she required what equaled an anvil to the skull to realize how intensely he wanted her.

It took a moment for her to gather a reply and it was maddeningly condescending when she did, "I hope you're better at surveillance and security than that. His hand was on my hip."

Oh yeah? Well, guess what? "It was migrating south like a flock of geese." He stood on one foot then the other, ever cognizant of his body's reaction to her appearance, "That's why I wanted to escort you. To keep these things from happening." He warily glanced over her again, "Good Lord, Sydney. Why are you dressed like this?"

Her lip pouted, obviously realizing it drove him nuts, "You don't like it?"

"That's the damn problem," he grumbled. "I love it and so does every other man in this room." He allowed himself a brief peek at her skirt and instantly regretted it thanks to his pulsing erection. He cringed in clear discomfort, "Are you wearing any panties under that thing?" The inflection sounded fatherly but his gaze was anything but.

She drew her hand softly along his jaw, "Guess."

A strangled noise eked past his throat and he clenched his jaw as she strode away, swaying her hips in time with the music. He growled, "I'm keeping an eye on you, woman. The way you look, I'll have to."

Watching her, Ethan grew angrier by the minute while his shorts grew smaller by the second. She drove him insane with desire and she loved it. When he got her home tonight, he'd show her just how insane he was about her and had been for sixteen years. "Down, boy," he grumbled at his erection. "We've got a long night ahead of us. I will get time with her, at least for some answers."

14

Sydney returned to the group, apologizing for the interruption. Ethan was right, of course. George's hand had been squarely on her ass, not her hip and it returned posthaste when she got within reach of him. A gentle squeeze on her backside sparked her anger but she bit it back, still watching Ethan from the corner of her vision. A voice from the side caught her attention, "Sydney, darling, you look fabulous!"

She automatically relaxed. Thank God. Now she could stop feeling so awkward. Jason's arm curled around her shoulders, gently urging her away from George, something she was grateful for. "You're a hit with everyone," her assistant gushed.

Sydney lightly rubbed her tush to rid herself of the disgusting feeling, "Yeah, and more of a hit than I wanted with *some* people," she grumbled with a pasted smile. Lecher was correct she reflected, giving George a friendly wave in response to his eager wink.

Jason noticed her uneasiness, "Honey, just tell him you're involved. George will back off, especially if he knows your sweetie is a police officer." He led her to the dessert table filled with every kind of sweet known to mankind. Cakes, pies, truffles, tortes, petite fours and even a Yule Log. Studying the latter, she noticed the phallic shape and pointed it out to Jason. He took one look and shrieked in laughter, "Well, we *are* about sex, darling."

The log entranced her temporarily, enough that Jason whispered, "Stare any longer and people might think you're a virgin."

Highly unlikely… Virgins probably didn't dress to feel the cold December breeze blowing across their behinds and into parts unknown. Sydney shivered at the remembrance. Even with the small jacket she'd worn inside, she felt the full effect of winter literally from top to bottom.

Jason poured two cups of punch for them. She briefly examined hers – it looked fruity, cherry maybe. She waited, allowing her assistant to guinea pig the first sip. He closed his eyes sighing deeply, "Oh, that's much better than last year's. Someone *finally* listened to me."

Feeling secure about the drink, Sydney took a small taste. The smooth fruity flavor – cherry, indeed – quickly gave way to pure scorching alcohol. Her eyes teared as the liquid bounced down her throat, into her stomach, lighting it aflame. Sydney's body flushed from her head to her now glowing toes. She gasped, "What is this? Moonshine?"

Jason laughed, "Maybe but it makes the party go rather well." He tugged at her elbow, "I see you have a puppy on his leash. Lead him, girl. Lead him."

She dabbed at her eyes, clearing them, then followed his pointing finger to Ethan. *He'd pursued her* to watch over her. A leash indeed. A little leather, a little lace, and a swing in her backyard was all it took. A devious smile curved her lips. Now if Pushkin was here, her life was complete. She'd searched the crowds for the man at the hospital but struck out every time. No one came close to the height, the build or voice. If she'd only seen his face…

Jason cheered her softly, "He's eating out of your hand, honey. I'll be surprised if you stay here another ten minutes before he sweeps you home and makes mad passionate love to you. Better eat something because it might be a while before you get the chance to eat again."

"I don't want to go home with Ethan. I want my admirer to sweep me off my feet," she knew she sounded like a child but, damn it, she was beginning to believe in fairytales again and wanted her white knight.

"Sydney, darling, take it where you can get it."

"Jason," was the whispered scold.

He shrugged, "Honey, I'm gay, I'm not dead and I know Ethan's on the edge." Happily gathering cakes and truffles, he handed her a small plate filled with delectable desserts, "Even if your admirer isn't here, you've got a sure thing with the lieutenant. When Pushkin reveals himself, you could have two men vying for your heart. Oh, the mere thought…"

Sydney still searched the crowd for a tall man with black hair. Still nothing. She resolved herself to partaking of the snack plate Jason assembled for her. She felt the heat of Ethan's gaze from across the room however the pang of desire winding through her chest and deep into her belly only applied to Pushkin. Before total disappointment settled in, she sipped her drink. Drowning her sorrows in moonshine seemed appropriate.

"So are you?" Jason asked.

Distractedly, she turned to him, "Am I what?"

"Are you ready for him to tear these clothes off and –"

"Hey, Sydney," a voice from behind interrupted Jason's question. She didn't readily recognize it and assumed it was another colleague. One thing for sure, it wasn't Pushkin. She gathered her senses and turned on one foot. She tossed a smile at the person then realized it was Ethan's partner, "John, I'm glad you joined us."

He returned the smile, "Difficult not to listen to you, especially dressed like that."

"It's warmer in here, at least. I was afraid you might be cold out there."

He moved closer, "Nope, I'm warming up real well now."

Sydney waved her hand across the display of food, "Take your pick. There is a great selection of food and drink. Though I'd stay away from the punch."

His blue eyes never left her, sweeping her body in the warmth of his gaze as it had before, only it felt more intense now, "Forget those. You're the only thing tempting me."

She nervously cleared her throat. Her assistant, hearing the exchange, rushed to concoct a diversion. The chorus of "Frosty The Snowman" blasted from the speakers as John stepped even closer. Sydney stepped back, her bottom brushing the edge of the table.

Jason's brow lowered, "Officer, try the Yule Log. It looks scrumptious…"

Sydney's incredulous expression met Jason, "Yule Log?"

Jason backtracked, near panic as she was. He stammered, obviously realizing the shape of the Yule Log, "Sorry, I meant the torte. The torte looks scrumptious and *it's down here*, Officer," he motioned to the end of the table. Jason glanced behind Sydney, his eyes popped wide, "Lord, honey. Here comes Santa Claus to the rescue."

She began to turn, wondering why the blood drained from his face. Something hard bumped her shoulder, jarring her forward nearly into Jason's arms. Sydney finally caught sight of Ethan barreling down on John, his tone as murderous as his frown, "What the hell are you doing?"

The commotion stunned everyone within viewing distance. Sydney had never seen Ethan so infuriated. His face crimson red, practically purple, and his body poised to attack and possibly maim.

John shrank back as Ethan towered over him, hands rolled into fists. Ethan's fierce temper unloaded on him like a dump truck. His large hands wrapped in John's coat, bringing him to eye level, "Making moves on Sydney will get you one thing. Hospitalized." His voice carried like thunder through the enormous auditorium, the warning intended for all the men who'd pawed "his woman" that night.

His booming voice handily silenced the room. Every person in attendance heard the outburst and they all turned to the scene unfolding before them, much to Sydney's embarrassment. A rush of heat flooded her cheeks and she just wanted to leave. Jason snugged his arm around her waist for support. The entire party ground to a halt except the music which started playing, "Merry Christmas, Baby."

John sputtered, "Ethan, I'm sorry –"

"Stay away from her." Ethan shook him hard once, "*She's mine.*"

"I am not *yours*," Sydney announced, astounded and outwardly offended that Ethan blatantly claimed her as his. Then she wished she'd kept her mouth shut. Ethan's head slowly raised, impaling her visually, "We'll see about that. Starting right now." He let go of his partner who scrambled not to tumble backwards.

Sydney backpedaled into Jason's embrace, apprehensive of her former lover's actions. Jason, however sturdy, couldn't compete with Ethan's strength but her assistant, by his hug, silently vowed to do his best. Ethan stopped in front of her calmly instructing, "Let her go."

"Ethan, you're embarrassing me," she stated while nodding toward the crowd of engrossed gawkers.

His hand wrapped firmly around her arm, pulling her free of Jason's hold. Her assistant managed to catch her other hand, "Honey, don't go if you're afraid. There are plenty of witnesses who can vouch to this brutality."

Ethan spun, nailing him with a glare, "She'll be fine. I just want to talk to her."

Sydney called him down, "For God's sake, Ethan. Grow up and let me g –"

He wheeled to her, freezing her to the spot, "And *you*. You've been asking for this all night."

Fingers snaked through her hair and closed in a fist. She let a short gasp as he brought his mouth down on hers. The kiss asked no permission nor showed any sign of ending until he felt her surrendering. Small timid sounds escaped her when he refused to stop sweetly assaulting her mouth. His tongue ravished her in ways that nearly made her tremble. He finally broke the deep kiss, his lips barely brushing hers, "I want you."

Her breaths emerged ragged and shaky, "If you remember, you've already had me."

He lightly kissed her again, "I'll never get enough of you. Let's go." He took her hand but she refused to budge. Ethan looked back, seeing the uncertainty on her face. A wicked smile split his face, "I'll do the caveman routine if you don't move along. Come to think of it, it *has* been a while since I've carried you over my shoulder." Then lowered his voice, "And seeing as how you aren't sufficiently covered under that skirt, I'd recommend you come along quietly."

And quietly she went – all the way to his car, all the way to his apartment, never uttering a word except "Yes" or "No" to his questions. Sydney didn't like the feelings rumbling inside her. They were threatening and dangerous to have and they weren't directed toward Ethan. Logan's image tormented her even as Ethan opened his apartment door and waved her in. "Why did you bring me here?" she asked, reluctant to shed her jacket.

"To work things out between us." He flipped on the light, his hand pressing tenderly on her back urged her inside, "And we *can* work things out."

Sydney focused on the centerpiece of the room. Ethan planned to bring her back tonight, obviously. His coffee table, once buried in

Penthouse and Playboys, now only held a blue Igloo cooler with a bottle of red wine shoved in the center of the ice. Beside the cooler sat two crystal glasses. The mere image of Ethan with crystal *anything* surprised her. In addition, he'd cleaned his apartment to immaculate perfection and placed a bouquet of wildflowers in the middle of the small dining table. She couldn't believe her eyes.

Ethan settled behind her, hands on her shoulders, "Have a drink with me."

"Just a drink? This looks like you've got other plans for us."

He eased the jacket down her arms then swept her hair back to press a soft kiss to the back of her neck, "Whatever you're comfortable with."

Sydney stiffened. She wasn't comfortable with the blatant move. Ethan always pushed, expecting her to merely accept and respond. In her younger days, she had. Now, however, her heart belonged to another man. His brother, and if either Calhoun found out, they'd both lynch her and sell tickets to the event. Ethan for supposed treachery and Logan for past sins.

With his "whatever you're comfortable with" comment, Ethan restricted her options mightily. Returning to the party was out, not that she felt comfortable with that. God knew her exit shocked enough people. She only hoped she still had a job Monday. Going home sounded best but he wouldn't allow it yet. Nevertheless, going any further than the talking stage was out, "I'll have a drink then I want to get my car and go home. I'm sick of leaving my car."

"It's beautiful, Syd. I'm envious of it."

"You wouldn't envy the amount I paid for it," she replied.

Ethan opened the wine and poured two glasses, "Hope you like this stuff. I asked Logan what a good brand was."

Logan. She cringed, feeling her stomach tighten then she purposefully shoved the eldest brother from her mind. Attending to Ethan's situation was paramount. Silently they settled on the couch until he mentioned, "You've really changed. I'd never have guessed you wearing this before."

Sydney sipped from the glass, noticing his attention focused on her mouth. This would be harder than she thought, "People change. I know I have." The faster she drank, the quicker she could leave.

Ethan sensed her intention and sat her glass on the coffee table, "Syd, I realize I hurt you," his hand stroked her arm as he sipped his wine, fortifying his courage. "That's why I've struggled so hard to connect with you again."

Sydney heard the pleading inflection, as his shaking hand touched her bare thigh. The muscles tightened, uneasy with his contact.

Covering his hand with hers, she spoke softly, "Ethan, I love you but not the same way you love me. Yes, you hurt me but there have been many years between then and now. I have to continue with my life past our chapter."

His grasp on her knee firmed and began sliding upward, "It's this other guy, isn't it?"

Stopping the ascent of his hand, she retrieved her glass and downed the rest of the wine, "Ethan, please listen to me. We had our chance and it didn't work. We were too young to commit to marriage, I know that now. We committed based on primal feelings, not true love."

The last of Ethan's hopeful expression fell. Sydney saw the heartbreak flood him. Memories of Logan's pained expression nagged at her. Ethan's mouth opened but said nothing. A barely imperceptible whisper emerged, "I loved you, baby. I still do. You loved me."

Turning him to her with a tender touch, she agreed, "You were my first love, Ethan and I was yours but things change."

Ethan held her hand in a gentle grasp, kissed the palm, "You've really changed. I mean, for the better and all, but you..." he paused, holding her hand to his cheek, obviously not wanting to let go, "you've changed. Independent, stubborn as blazing hell..."

"Ah," her velvety voice responded with a chuckle, "and you're not."

He smiled a little then reached for the wine bottle. Tilting it to his glass, she noticed his trembling hands. Sydney stretched to steady the bottle but it slipped from his grasp. The bottle tipped and red wine spilled on her blouse and skirt. Sydney gasped with surprise as cold wine chilled her breasts, stomach and lap.

Ethan groaned while scrambling off the couch, "Syd, I'm so sorry. I didn't mean to –"

"It was an accident. If you'll get some towels, I'll take care of it."

He rushed to the kitchen cabinet for dishtowels and before she realized it, his hand pressed a towel to her breasts then sank to her lap in a hurried attempt to soak up the wine. Sydney stopped him, "I'll handle this, okay? Thanks."

Ethan looked on with heavy regret, "I feel awful for spilling it on you."

"Accidents happen. If I could just borrow some clothes, you can take me home."

"I'll grab some sweats and a shirt for you," he raced into the bedroom.

Sydney knew he hadn't spilled the wine on purpose. Her speech rattled him, evidently to the core. His hands trembled, his voice shook, his ego injured. If he faced the truth, he knew their relationship past friends was history. However, Ethan Calhoun prohibited surrender. In many ways, he'd have made the ideal Custer.

He rounded the corner extending a pair of gray Atlanta Police Department sweatpants and a white t-shirt reading "I'm with Stupid." He shrugged sheepishly, "I figured the shirt was appropriate tonight. Throw these and my duty jacket on and I'll take you home. I'll make sure your car gets home safely too."

Ethan's manner and words were sweeter than pure sugar. His acceptance of her decision surpassed any hopes she'd imagined – if he honestly accepted it. She headed to the bathroom, kissing his cheek on the way, "Thank you."

Closing the bathroom door, she debated over showering first but then realized being naked in Ethan's shower right now invited trouble. As the phone began ringing, she quickly skinned out of the tight leather skirt then unbuttoned the wet silk blouse. Well, so much for sex bomb.

Convinced the leather mini-skirt wasn't her style anyway, she decided to ditch the look all together. It was a nice temporary change but not a permanent one.

"Syd," he called from the hallway, "I gotta go. Captain's called out some off-duty officers to help with traffic control downtown. I don't know for how long so make yourself at home, okay?"

She sighed. Why not? The evening certainly hadn't been picture perfect yet so why should it change? "Sure. Be careful, Ethan."

"I will. And, Syd? If I'm not back pretty soon, just pile up in my bed. The sheets are clean."

She nearly laughed. He worried about her sleeping on clean sheets, "I hadn't a doubt about it. See you when you get home."

15

A constant knocking on the door awoke Ethan. Who the hell was it at this time of morning? With Sydney snuggled against him, her head cradled on his shoulder, he hated to crawl out of bed so he didn't. Glancing past Sydney, the second hand on the clock slowly rose to ten o'clock. Arriving home at three assured Sydney would be long asleep, a fact he cursed over and over. It had been years since he'd been relegated to traffic cop – it figured he'd be called out the night he had Sydney at his place. He'd trudged in, followed the dark room by memory until standing in his doorway. When he saw her lying in his bed, silhouetted in the moonlight, he realized her speech about primal feelings made complete sense. He felt extremely primal right then.

As quietly as humanly possible, he'd stripped off his clothes then edged closer to the bed and slowly sat down. The bed creaked and sank with his weight, causing him to hold his breath. Sydney stirred but still slept so he eased down until lying beside her. Surprisingly, she snuggled against his bare chest, her arm hugging him close. Ethan willed his heart to stop pounding. This was too good to be true. She basically crawled next to him, her hair tickling his shoulder and ribs, her body heat warming him. Ethan heard her mumbling and leaned closer, whispering, "What is it, Syd?"

Her lips barely moved and all Ethan caught was something sounding like "Hold me." He happily did.

Now, at ten o'clock, he wanted more than to hold her. He inhaled her scent, the faint flowery smell of her hair. Then he felt her snuggle closer to him, wrapping herself into him. He never wanted this moment to end but the knocking refused to subside. Ethan's temper flared as he softly tickled her arm. Sleepily her eyes floated open, trying to focus.

His anger evaporated at the tiny smile on her face – and she hadn't even made eye contact yet. This morning was shaping up well. He smiled too, "Hey there, sugar."

Sydney's expression pinched and she blinked once, twice. "Ethan?" The name poured thick like molasses.

"That's me, babe." He touched her cheek, lifting her mouth to his. His lips brushed hers and recognition finally dawned as she pulled back, "What happened? Why are you in bed with me?" The confusion cleared slowly but eventually memories of the previous night clicked into place. "Oh. What time did you get back?"

"About three." Ethan noticed she backed away from him slightly now. So what was all the cuddly, sweet stuff during the night? Who did she think she was with?

She yawned, "Someone's banging on your door."

"Yes, and I'll go take care of them. You need to rest and when I get back, we're having our talk because I'm fixing us breakfast."

She didn't bother to argue, he noticed as he swung the covers back and made his way to the front door.

Suddenly the anger reappeared. Whoever the hell was at his door was about to find out the definition of "wrath". Rounding the living room, he picked up speed to stop the maniacal pounding. The door yanked open and he stood breathing fire at… "Logan?"

"Howdy, bro. Busy?"

"Yes, extremely. Come back later." Ethan swung the door closed but Logan pushed his way in. "Can't. I've only got today off and wanted an update on your plans with Sydney."

"Shh, for God's sake," he growled.

Logan didn't pick up on the meaning, "Why are you shushing me? You're the one who said you had a great plan for getting her back. Did it work?" He continued on his way to the kitchen, unaffected by Ethan's efforts to redirect him to the door, "And if so, how in hell did you get her to listen rationally after what happened with Amanda?"

Ethan planted himself immediately in front of him, fists on his hips and blazing a glare that could melt glass. He ground the words between clenched teeth while pointing in his bedroom, "She's in my bed right now, Logan. Don't screw this up for me. It's taken me *sixteen years* to get her back."

A brief but strong wave of nausea rolled through Logan's gut. Syd was in Ethan's bed? Once shock gave way to logic, Logan found it difficult to believe the scene unfolded the way Ethan described. Maybe Sydney fell and knocked herself out leaving Ethan no choice but tuck her into his bed. Maybe her apartment complex was being fumigated and he was the only one offering a place to stay. Maybe... Oh hell, "Ethan, has she said she's staying with you, as in a relationship?"

Ethan squirmed, giving Logan his answer. His brother tried to lie but Logan always discovered the truth, "That's what I thought."

"Look, a little more time, that's all I need. And if you'll leave..."

Logan decided to ride this for all its worth. His dark brows quirked, "She's in your bed, huh? Awake or asleep?"

"Hopefully, asleep. Although at this rate it's doubtful."

"I can only see Syd getting into your bed if she had no choice." Logan's eyes bugged in mock disgust, "You villain. You didn't tie that woman to the bed and coerce her." Playing off his brother's flustered state, he persisted by walking toward the bedroom, "Now that would be worth seeing. Yes, indeed."

Ethan strutted against his brother, chest to chest, his nostrils flared, "Don't make me hit you."

Logan snorted at his brother's show, "Cool down, hot stuff. I just want to see what I'm missing." He took a step around him. Two strides later, he stood at Ethan's bedroom door and caught a glimpse of Sydney sleeping, her hair splayed across the pillow, the sheet tucked modestly beneath her arms.

From the short distance, Logan saw how the sheet accented her graceful curves, long legs and trim waist and those ample breasts. His hands itched to touch them, his mouth craved to taste them. His sex thickened and his throat went instantly dry, "Damn but she's beautiful."

Ethan's chest swelled with obvious pride while he leaned against the door jamb. Logan couldn't draw his vision away from her, nor did he want to.

"You know," Ethan reminded, "she wasn't unattractive in high school as you recall."

"My recollection is fine." His eyes greedily roamed her body, soaking in as many details about her as possible. Even sleeping she aroused his primal hunger, "Age certainly becomes that woman."

Ethan shrugged his weight to both feet to assume a wary stance, "Behave, Logan. You weren't interested in her in high school – if you recall."

His brother was certifiable if he actually believed that. Without confirming or denying he answered, "As I said, my recollection is fine."

Ethan stepped in front of him again, this time drawing the bedroom door shut to give her privacy. Logan stopped him, "So what if she wakes up? I'd like to see her sashay in here modeling a sheet. If it's wrapped just right, it accentuates a woman..." he pointed to a certain area. An area his tongue and teeth hungered after.

Ethan boiled beneath the surface, "You won't be seeing that part of her."

"On the contrary, your apartment is slightly chilly," he winked, "and that's all it takes." Logan saw his brother tense from head to toe, "Ethan, you look like a rooster."

Ethan looked close to tearing his hair out, "Why are you here? I could be in bed 'accentuating' Sydney right now, you know."

"If she'll let you. These days she's finicky about her accentuating partners, I'm sure."

Ethan took his brother's arm and dragged him away from the bedroom door and into the kitchen. Sighing, Logan resigned himself to a barstool while Ethan rattled a frying pan out of the cabinet. Ah, breakfast. Unless his brother unexpectedly acquired a chef's talent, Sydney's stay would be brief at most. Logan remembered the last meal Ethan prepared. Once the smoke cleared, Logan elected to eat at the hospital, leaving Ethan with a swarm of put-off firefighters telling him there was a reason for McDonald's. Poor Syd, Logan mused.

Ethan moved to the coffee pot then stopped. Thinking a moment, he finally asked, "Does she drink coffee?"

Logan shrugged, "Might as well brew some. Drag out the Wild Turkey too, because once she realizes she's in your bed, she may need fortification."

Ethan scowled, "That's real funny." Then he sat three coffee cups on the bar, "You're too cynical. That's why you're not married."

Logan *knew* why he wasn't married. His heart belonged to only one woman. Suddenly he heard stirrings in the bedroom. Sydney must have heard them talking. He really hoped she'd model that sheet for him. A few short seconds later, she emerged, her hair askew and sleepily rubbing her eyes as she yawned. She was not wearing a sheet. Instead she wore Ethan's white "I'm with Stupid" t-shirt and a pair of his boxers. Yellow boxers with happy faces. Logan's grin broadened, the irony not lost on him. Even wearing those ugly boxers, she was still sexy as hell. "Mornin', Sunshine," he called, presenting a thoroughly wicked smile.

Sydney halted in her tracks at the deep voice. Glancing up, her eyes widened at the man in jeans and Atlanta Hawks sweatshirt sitting at the bar. His ravenous gaze stroked her from head to toe and back to her face. "Hi," she squeaked, her toes curling into the carpet. She obviously didn't recognize him but, he noticed, she didn't dart out of sight either. She did, however, follow his gaze to her chest. Because of the chill in the room, her breasts were tight, the nipples on high alert.

Logan visually plundered the woman across the room. The moment she saw him, Sydney acquired the deer in the headlights stance and sported it well. It gave him plenty of time to admire her natural beauty and fully appreciate those plump breasts with the dark, petite nipples poking against the cotton. "Mmm…" He rolled in a low tone, "Can they come out and play?"

Seeing where his brother's attention lingered, Ethan smacked Logan's head with a spatula, "Shut up or she'll hear you. And if she does, you'll deal with me."

Sydney seemed shocked at Ethan's sudden attack. Clearly she hadn't heard them. Her vision remained on Logan though she addressed Ethan, "I'm taking a shower while you visit."

Ethan nodded, "Okay, sugar. I'll have breakfast for us shortly. We'll eat *alone*."

Logan watched Sydney return to the bedroom. The sway of her cute ass covered in happy faces was nearly more than he could bear. "That wasn't subtle at all, bro. I know when I'm not welcome."

"No, you don't or you'd already be gone." He leaned across the bar, resting on his elbows, "Stop ogling my woman."

"I'm admiring, Ethan. There's a difference. And she hasn't said she's yours." He spotted her once more as she emerged, this time rounding the corner slowly. She looked at Logan then his brother, "I need some clean clothes."

Ethan meandered into the bedroom, "Just look in the top and second drawer, babe. Plenty of stuff to choose from. We'll drop by your place later on, okay?"

Stifling a chuckle, Logan poured himself a cup of coffee, "What happened to her own clothes? I assume she was wearing some when she entered the apartment." Suddenly the voices in the bedroom dropped to whispers – no doubt she spoke of him now. Good. He never wanted Sydney to forget him though he was convinced she hadn't recognized him yet. Sure enough, he saw her peer guardedly around the corner like an inquisitive little girl. He waved, "Peek-a-boo, Syd."

"Logan," she acknowledged warily. "How are you?"

He noted her businesslike manner and rewarded her with a cheerful response, "Much better, especially this morning, thank you. And you?"

"I'm doing very well, thanks."

Logan hopped off the barstool and neared her. Her wide, green eyes zeroed in on him, her head tilted severely back to meet his gaze. Standing so close their bodies nearly touched, Sydney would fit comfortably in his arms with plenty of room to rest his chin on top of her head.

Logan saw her clasping two pairs of boxers in her hand. He also noticed she looked much as she had in sixth grade before he kissed her. Startled and unsure of him. He studied each pair of boxers then plucked one from her hand, "These."

"Excuse me?" she asked hoarsely and right away cleared her throat. Her parted lips invited him to kiss her – something he wished he could do. His eyes sparkled, "Wear this pair after you shower." Then he lightly tugged the yellow boxers on her hips, making her gasp and reach to hold them up. He finished, "I'm sure we'll all appreciate them more than these hideous monsters."

"You won't be here after she showers," Ethan effectively sandwiched Sydney between the brothers. Two hands eased around her belly from behind and Ethan whispered, "Run along, babe. Breakfast will be ready soon." Sweeping her hair to the side, he pressed a kiss to the nape of her neck. Sydney swallowed, her unease written in her expression. Then she jumped as Ethan's palm smacked her rear. The action accidentally thrust her hips against Logan who reacted merely with a slow blink and a sigh. His body responded to the brief contact and he released his aggravation on Ethan, "She's not your property. Have some manners." He looked at her, "Don't let him get away with that, Syd."

She glared back at Ethan, promising, "I won't." Restlessness bloomed in her demeanor now that Ethan's obsessive side reared its ugly head.

Logan noticed the longer she remained sandwiched between them, the more anxious she grew. He, however, reveled in her soft warmth against him. Her heat along with her body aligning with his, her breasts pressing against his chest nearly drove him to take drastic measures. His self control ran on empty while the pulsing desire in his pants begged him to follow through on his wishes. Luckily, common sense stepped in while he vowed that stepping *aside* wasn't an option for him. If someone moved, it would be Ethan and he knew damn well his brother was rooted to the floor.

Logan could tell she forced direct eye contact with him, "And to set this story straight, *nothing happened* last night except Ethan abducted me *again* and accidentally spilled wine all over my clothes. He was called out on business and since I didn't have a car, I slept here alone most of the night."

Just the thought of her with Ethan turned his gut. Why she appeared so flustered, he didn't know then he took note of his expression. It was as sour as his stomach, "Thanks for the update. I'm sure Ethan will still try to jump you though. Unless you want to wear him home as well, stripping down for any reason wouldn't be prudent."

She blinked, speechless. She didn't even react when Ethan swung his fist at Logan's shoulder and nailed it solidly. Logan couldn't look away from her, especially with her budding wounded expression. He had sounded bitter to the core and she'd picked up on it. Scrambling mentally to repair the damage, he offered, "I'll take you home."

"Like hell you will," Ethan argued. "She's my guest."

"Only because you pickled her clothes after hauling her off against her will. I tremble to think how many laws you've broken since she's come back..." Well, damn. That didn't come out right either. Frustrated with his inability to communicate, Logan shoved his hand through his hair, "Syd, just let me take you home."

She slid from between the two and headed to the bathroom, "That's okay. I'll let Ethan do it. We agreed to it last night. But thanks."

Logan knew by her tone he'd hurt her. His intention wasn't to accuse her of not having morals or common sense and he certainly didn't want her to think she was the cause of Ethan's current lawbreaking spree but that's how it appeared and she took it to heart.

She took only long enough to stop and quietly say, "Good to see you again, Logan."

He turned, still admiring her even as she stepped in the bathroom and began closing the door. He forced himself to speak – and carefully, "You too, Syd, and I'm sorry for..." The door shut, reducing the last of his comment to a whisper, "hurting your feelings." His scrubbed his palm against his jaw, angry with himself, "That's the one thing I never wanted to do."

Sydney heard Logan loud and clear, at least the "sorry for" portion and she couldn't stomach hearing the rest. He'd already implied things that made her color to the point her ears glowed like neon signs. If Logan wanted to humiliate her, he'd done a proper job. She not only felt cheap but stupid. Topping her mortification like a fat, juicy cherry was his reference to her causing Ethan to fall off the "sane" wagon. If he remembered correctly, Ethan *never* exhibited normal behavior in his life. But as usual, once Logan made up his mind, nothing or no one could change it.

So when he began another barrage with his "I'm sorry", she couldn't shut the door fast enough. Then she spent a good deal of time leaned against the cabinet, breathing deeply to regain her bearings. Being surrounded by the Calhoun boys again was enough to overwhelm a girl. They both acted like teenagers at times. Age certainly hadn't curtailed that aspect of them. But the years finely tuned their outer attractiveness. Even Logan hadn't changed except for a few laugh lines at the corners of his eyes. He was still exceptionally handsome like Ethan. The brothers favored with their dark eyes and black curly hair. Both kept their hair short enough for the ladies to luxuriate in the softness by running their fingers through the waves. They mutually boasted mile wide shoulders and skyscraper height though Logan was taller than Ethan by a few inches. Their personalities opposed in some degrees. Ethan tended to be domineering while Logan's sweetness preyed on her dreams more and more – at least until today. He'd sounded downright condescending and hateful. That told her he not merely smarted from her rejection years ago but boiled over it.

He was the definition of gentle giant but didn't hesitate to utilize his physical size to his benefit. When a person refused to agree with Logan's point of view, his hands went to his hips, giving him a killer wingspan – all while he used the calmest tone to persuade someone, or command them, whichever was required.

Sydney started the shower and stripped down. Looking at her reflection in the full length mirror, she nearly screamed. Her hair tangled in every direction and she looked positively hideous. No wonder Logan bit her head off. She'd look better without one.

She stepped in the shower, letting the warm water course over her. Remembering the night before, she'd retired at midnight, crawling in Ethan's bed. Sometime during the night she recalled the bed moving, a masculine body touching hers. And she hugged that body close, caressing it, and called him Logan. Logan! Oh God, had Ethan heard her? Had she said it loud enough for him to hear? She prayed not but his overzealous actions moments earlier could have been a clue he *had* heard her.

Sydney still heard the men talking outside the bathroom. As the moments passed, their voices moved into the kitchen again. Even with the hiss of water she could distinguish between the two men's voices. Ethan's calmness sporadically lifted with excitement. Logan's similar calm tone varied with periods of clipped replies and humorless statements. Though she couldn't decipher the words, she knew they were talking about her. About the past. She'd turned Logan down years ago and if he felt slightly vindictive, he merely had to tell Ethan what transpired the day she found Amanda and Ethan together. Season it with a few half-truths and lies and presto, Ethan's temper would explode all over her and no shower would help her then. After the previous few minutes with Logan, she wouldn't put anything past him.

16

The New Year was barely a week old. Atlanta saw its first snow of the year – eight inches. Just enough to muck up the roads, sidewalks and people's temperaments. Sydney left her apartment extra early that morning to compensate for the weather. Creeping to a stop for a red light, she saw more flakes beginning to fall. The forecast appeared dismal for drivers. Two or three more inches by nightfall ensured icy, basically impassable roads for the following day.

The red Camaro handled well in the snow to her surprise. This was the second snowstorm she'd driven in since she owned it. The car she drove prior to it, an early model Ford Taurus sedan proved better on the stuff but Georgia rarely received enough snow to worry with. After scrimping and saving, she'd finally been able to afford the '99 Camaro SS Coupe – used but still in prime shape. It was a gem with T-Tops, LS1 350 HP engine, a monsoon stereo system with 12 disc cd player and best of all, very low mileage and it was meticulously maintained. Sydney swung an arrangement with the dealer to hold the car for two months while she paid in installments. It hadn't hurt that she was dating his son at the time. Unfortunately, the relationship didn't work out but the

Camaro had. From the time she drove it off the lot she babied the car. Her sister hated it, complaining about its unsafe design and the fact Camaros were popular with thieves even with their anti-theft devices. There were ways around those systems, Sam said, and some day a thief might knock her in the head for that "obnoxiously expensive" car. Sydney waved off her lectures as jealousy. Regrettably, her Coupe didn't have an anti-theft system but did have Pass Key protection. The engine wouldn't start without the Pass Key and, she informed Sam, she was very cognizant of her surroundings while out.

She arrived at work twenty minutes early and once safely in her office, took time to watch the snow fall. More flurries drifted past the window, larger flakes now, she noticed. Jason whistled his way in and placed a stack of papers on her desk, "These need reviewing and signing before day's end."

Thumbing indifferently through each group, Sydney mumbled, "Okay."

Jason paused while surveying her mood. Softly, he inquired if something had happened. In the same tone she replied, "Not yet but I'm meeting Ethan for lunch."

He watched her trace the edge of a manuscript thoughtfully. "What's happening at lunch?"

Finally her vision met his and she allowed a tense smile through, "He still thinks there's hope for us. He won't believe me so today I'm trying *again* to make it final." Sifting through the monstrous stack he lugged in, Sydney amassed three smaller, more manageable ones. He perched himself on her desk, leaning in,   "Honey, he won't like it but you're doing the right thing."

Sydney blinked, amazed at Jason's bluntness, "Really?"

Now more animated, he waved his hands as if shooing a fly, "Absolutely. You're way too stressed with Ethan. Look at you, honey. And that possessiveness, you know. Not good. Everyone was fraught with concern when you left the party with him that night. Sydney, you need a nurturing, loving partner, one who doesn't take note of your every move – well, unless he's *admiring* your every move. Go to lunch, be firm with Ethan, leave and don't look back. Put your energy into Pushkin. He eventually will reveal himself."

She cranked his words through her muddled mind. For days she'd battled, planned and mentally prepared herself for this eventuality. Ethan hadn't accepted her decision which forced her into harsher measures. Measures she dreaded. After a few moments, she patted his hand, "You deserve a raise."

Jason hopped down and rounded the desk. Throwing his arms around her lovingly, he bubbled, "The doctor is always in for you, darling." Before exiting her office a sly grin slowly crept across his cheeks, "And I'll be looking for that gratuity in my next check."

Sydney was about to reply when the phone rang, demanding her attention, "Sydney Eatonton,"

"Hey, sugar, why don't I pick you up for lunch? The roads are a mess and your car isn't exactly built for this stuff."

Ethan's voice made her stomach twist. His offer, however sweet, wouldn't derail her objective, "I drove to work, didn't I?"

"Okay, I *want* to pick you up because I've got a surprise for you."

Automatically her face pinched with angst. He wasn't making this easy but she hadn't expected him to. She suspected the day would get much worse before it got better. Ethan stepped into her life and felt possessed to stomp around in it. Looking up, she saw Jason pointing to the phone mouthing, "Be firm." Inwardly, she repeated it to herself and nodded. "You shouldn't have, Ethan. I –"

"You deserve it. You put up with my bizarre nature so you should have this. Now I'll be there about eleven thirty. Meet me out front."

One deep breath later, she answered, "No. Frisco's isn't but a few blocks over and I'll meet you there."

Concern laced his tone, "Something's on your mind. You want to meet now?"

She wanted to, yes. Anything to get this over with. She checked her schedule just as Jason stepped closer. "Jason, can these papers wait an hour? Ethan wants to meet now."

"Go, honey," he whispered, "get it done. I'll hold down the fort."

She mouthed a thank you and answered Ethan, "Meet me in ten minutes, okay?"

"I'll be there. And Syd? I love you."

She nearly groaned. This was getting harder by the second. "I'll see you shortly, Ethan." She hung up and thanked Jason profusely for his help. He gathered her purse for her, his hand supportively on her shoulder, "Just remember it's best for both of you. Take a deep breath and focus. Think of Pushkin."

"Pushkin, right," she absently agreed, allowing Jason to steering her out the door and into the elevator. She checked her watch, "I have a manuscript in my car. I need it sent upstairs today –"

"Consider it done. I'll go down with you and you can pitch it at me as you drive off."

On the ride down, Jason offered more advice. Before exiting the elevator, he faced her and swept her hair behind her shoulders. His assuring, almost apologetic smile, made her frown ease. With another encouraging hug, he finished, "Ethan's a nice fellow but he's just not right for you."

A weak smile emerged, "You sound like my family, only they'd have left out the 'nice fellow' part." Two steps out of the elevator, her shoulders slumped, "Great. I left my coat upstairs."

"I'll go back for it," he offered.

She waved it off, "No, it's a short jaunt to the car and the drive isn't too far. I just want this done." She told Jason to stay inside and she'd run after the manuscript. He stayed in the foyer chatting with the doorman while watching her brave the elements, keys in hand.

She hurried to the Camaro which was parked beside the building in a small parking area for employees. Normally she parked in a space facing Peachtree but due to weather, those filled quickly.

On her way to the car, she hopped over some slick patches of pavement and baby-stepped over others. One more glance at her watch told her she had five minutes maximum to grab the manuscript and beat it to Frisco's in time to meet Ethan. Reaching to slide the key in the lock, she was surprised when the door suddenly opened on its own. It slammed her backwards, throwing her into a flailing fight to remain standing on the slippery surface. Struggling to stay upright, she released the keys to clutch at the hood, her fingers clawing to get a solid grip. They finally caught on the edge near the windshield wipers.

In that time a memory flashed in her panicked brain. She'd forgotten to lock her car. After nearly slipping on the ice that morning, she pushed the door closed without remembering to lock it first.

Now she faced a man looking like the winner of the World Weight Lifting Championship. Gathering his leather jacket at his waist, he stood tall over the car and her. Sydney stared into an ominous, angry expression. His stubble-shadowed jaw set hard and two dark, deep-set eyes drilled her as viciously as his voice, "Gimme the keys or you're dead."

It took Sydney a brief moment to evaluate her situation and even less time to make the wrong decision. Granted, his bulk and appearance weren't favorable to contest but she refused to have her car stolen. She tipped her chin back, showing much less fear than she felt coursing inside, "You're not taking my car." She felt like David taking on Goliath. A thieving Goliath that wasn't making off with her Camaro, except she hadn't one weapon at her aid, not even a flimsy slingshot. Except... She spied her purse next to her feet and bent to retrieve it.

As though reading her mind, his face darkened and the bulging muscles in his arms flexed, "Big mistake, bitch."

Sydney promptly discovered his meaning when the door crashed against her head, sending her to her knees. One hand cradled her head as the other fumbled for the cell phone. Then she spotted the car keys jutting from the ice. He scrambled to grab them as she lunged. Two hands gripped the silver angel medallion in unison. Sydney's left hand joined her right in the pulling tussle, covering it to add to her grasping power. The man's knee nailed her left wrist, grinding the tender flesh into the jagged ice until her hand opened, a mere whimper escaping her lips. Her right hand stayed tight around the angel, struggling to reclaim her keys.

The traffic along Peachtree moved at a steady snail's pace with a few drivers voicing their displeasure via their car's horn. Sydney briefly reflected that had she been able to park in her usual spot, those ticked off commuters might have noticed the scuffle taking place around her Camaro. As it were, she fought for her life in a remote part of Fantasy's parking lot surrounded by pickups and SUVs.

She held tight to the medallion until a slicing pain ripped across her forearm. Her hand opened almost immediately and she jerked her wounded arm from beneath the door, cradling it like an animal appraising the source of its pain. With the wound flowing with blood, she felt vaguely woozy. Thick red drops fell onto her slacks and mingled in the ice and snow. The warm blood spread into an increasingly larger stain on the fabric, and she pressed her hand on the wound, applying pressure. Then she looked up. He glared at the huddled heap on the other side of the door, the switchblade playing between his fingers then he folded his large frame into the driver's seat and started the car.

In a last attempt to save her prized Camaro, she scrambled to her feet and rounded the door. Before she could reach in, she saw the car shudder and she recognized the click of the transmission changing gears.

He'd shifted the Camaro into Reverse and with the cumbersome door still wide open, it was going to knock her down if she didn't move.

She wheeled to escape the moving car. Racing over the slick pavement, she heard the Camaro's powerful engine roar as it gained speed and the tires crunched across ice. A sudden jarring blow spun her, stole her balance and ripped a cry from deep within her soul.

The door's edge had solidly clipped her right hip and as she collapsed, the side of her head struck the ground, literally causing her to see stars. It finally occurred to her that fighting for the Camaro might have indeed proved fatal. Through clouded vision, she noticed the car propelled her backwards a considerable distance. Between her head, arm and back, they agonizingly described how damaging the overall struggle had been. Then she saw it – a wall of red closing in on her. The car *still* backed toward her, the tires and license plate nearing at a frightening pace. The brake lights abruptly blinked then stayed solid to stop the car backward slide. The Camaro, however, continued skimming effortlessly toward her. Sydney tried to move but pain crippled her. With each effort, her right hip and leg radiated agony to blackout levels. At the rate she inched herself along, crying out with every minor advance, it was impossible to escape the large, heavy car. Her mind clambered for a solution but instead opted for a sincere prayer. *God, please stop that car...*

The Camaro shifted into driving gear and slid a few additional feet backward even as the thief floored the accelerator. The car swung wildly from side to side, sending pelting her with of ice shards. Shielding her face with her good arm, she tried to move, to stand up, but cried out again. Flakes of snow kissed her tear-streaked face as a chill raked her.

Her body felt colder than the ice she laid on. Her thoughts wavered between losing her precious car to praying Jason or anyone noticed something wrong. She needed help and her purse laid twenty feet away. Retrieving it herself equaled an Olympic feat and would take forever – if she even succeeded. Her fuzzy mind attempted to crank out a solution then finally gave up, surrendering to sleep. Her eyes gently closed, resigning herself that sleep cured this level of intense pain.

Through a long, faraway tunnel, she heard Jason's shrill scream, "Sydney! Oh my God, honey. Wake up. *Wake up!*"

She thought she managed another groan for an answer. Through the same tunnel, she heard him scramble around her, carefully navigating the slick parking lot to her purse, "Don't worry. I'm calling 911. Just stay with me, honey."

17

Amid the clatter of metal and loud chatter of voices, a familiar voice floated into her semi-conscious brain, "What have we got?" The calm, sexy timbre soothed her unlike Jason's frantic tone. The EMTs hadn't proved any better. Calling out numbers and names of drugs in a rapid fire manner made her ache worse, made her worry. Jason rode in the ambulance with her, trying to calm her and provide the EMTs with information. He also recited a terrifying list of possible injuries, scaring the daylights out of her. Being unable to move – or to slap Jason senseless – agitated her more. The EMTs strapped her to a backboard and immobilized her head, preventing the concept of a simple wiggle, much less assault. Thankfully, as Jason prattled on, the EMTs at last shushed him while they worked, taking vitals, starting an IV. She exhaustively answered questions thrown her way, at least until sleep crept in. Then, like magic, Jason's shrieking heralded her awake, a noise not unlike an all-girl's soprano rendition of the Hallelujah Chorus.

The gurney ride from ambulance to emergency room felt similar to riding a horse – a three legged horse. The initial blast of cold air brought her fully awake however briefly. But, as though the EMTs refused – like Jason – to let her rest, they took the roughest path possible over the pavement and bumps into the noisy but warm emergency entrance. *Finally, now I can sleep...*

The doctor's voice sounded familiar to her, however, and as he continued talking, her aching brain unsuccessfully flipped through a mental rolodex of names. His rich, serene voice nearly lulled her to sleep. She felt herself drifting again, yielding to the pounding headache, as he asked questions and responded in kind using the same tone. Even as the EMTs reeled off her age, how they found her, possible injuries, and what had happened according to her, she felt herself floating, giving in to her body's wishes.

Jason suddenly and frantically yelled, "Wake up, honey! No sleeping!"

Sydney jerked, cried out miserably from the sudden movement then felt two pairs of warm hands gently pat hers, assuring her everything was all right.

"Pipe down, loudmouth," the doctor replied. "If you can't restrain yourself, leave. Yelling only upsets the patient *and* the doctor." He was faced away from her but she wished he would keep talking. He sounded calm, in control, "Vitals?"

Her arms and legs didn't feel as restricted now but she felt her clothes systematically being cut off then a quick pain in her arm. Since she already had an IV, she assumed they took blood. She wanted to protest that instead of sucking blood from her, they should be pumping pain medication *into* her.

Sydney heard a calm reply to the doctor's request as the voice recited her blood pressure and heart rate, the latter evidently registering higher than normal.

"Mostly because of the *noise*," was the doctor's pointed reference. Jason immediately apologized but the doctor sounded thoroughly peeved, "You have no business in here. Step outside and I'll talk to you later."

Another chill raked her near-naked body. Jason wrung his hands nervously, beseeching the doctor to let him stay, and promising to stay quiet. Sydney knew Jason meant well. A fact the doctor seemed to either overlook or disregard, "You're disturbing me and the patient," and added a firm conclusion, "so out."

Sydney groaned for a blanket. She was freezing with only her panties and bra. "Hold on, sweetie," a pleasant female voice said. The nurse continued talking to her as though Sydney was fully capable of conversing, "We need the rest of your clothes then I'll cover you." She felt cold metal slide under the seam of her panties and another under her bra. Both disappeared in record time. For some reason her modesty evaporated. She just wanted out of pain. The harder it set in, the colder she got. The sweat forming on her face and body chilled her, making her shiver. The pain etched into her bones and she voiced another plea for relief except no one apparently listened.

Jason called to her, "Sydney, don't worry about a thing. I'll let Ethan know right away."

"Sydney?" The doctor's tone rose questioningly, "Ethan?" As the voice neared she detected solid recognition in it, "Oh my God."

"You know her?" Jason asked, his voice hopeful.

"I certainly do," was the unsettled response.

Sydney's heart monitor ran amuck while she battled toward consciousness. She now knew the doctor's name. She also knew the car should have squashed her. It would have been more merciful.

Barely feeling herself rise from the depths, she struggled until her eyes fluttered open and she groaned. Logan Calhoun filled her vision, commanding in a deep voice, "Calm down, Sydney. I won't have you dying in my care."

Sydney tried to follow orders. But his grim appearance looming over her didn't exactly promote relaxation. Memories of fists hitting trees, of him yelling at her, flooded back along with memories of his angered expression flavored with bitter hurt when she refused him years ago. Added to that were memories of his coolness and extreme formal manner weeks ago at Ethan's apartment. Yes, the car should have mashed her. Sydney put great effort into speaking but only sputtered a whisper. Logan bent closer, "Say again, Syd?"

His ear lingered within an inch of her lips as she whispered, "Stay away from me."

Logan nearly grinned at her plea. Poor Syd. What she must think of him. Sixteen years obviously couldn't erase a tantrum thrown in a haze of desire. The same hands that battered the forty year-old oak now had to repair the woman who witnessed them do it. Sydney shied from him that day at Ethan's place – even avoided him by holding up in the bathroom. Now she had no choice but let him touch her. Logan cleared his throat, directing his thoughts to the pained expression beneath him and not the pained intensity of his need for her.

He returned the favor of grazing her ear with his lips, whispering,

"I can't do that, sweetheart. You're injured and in my emergency room. Let me see what's going on and what I can do about it."

"That's why I don't want you touching me. I won't live through it."

Logan stood up, chuckling while snapping on a pair of gloves, "I'm actually pretty good at playing doctor. Now you get to see how good." Turning to a nurse, he instructed, "Make a note that she's awake and alert enough to insult the attending physician."

From his initial assessments, he knew she suffered from shock. Her color faded to a pallid color as a sheen of sweat formed on her skin. The moment he touched her throat he noticed her eyes widened with fear. Logan shook his head and said with a hint of humor, "I'm here to help, not hurt you, Syd." His humor faded when he noticed how cool her skin felt.

Logan watched Sydney blink several times, her eyes uncertain about either focusing or staying shut. He rounded the table to examine the wound on her head, "You really didn't need another hole in your head." His humor brought a tiny smile from her and he patted her shoulder, "Soon as I finish the exam, I'll take care of this, and we'll get a CT scan, some x-rays and see where to go from there."

"I hurt," was the trembling response.

Logan's brow furrowed as he noticed tears pooling in her eyes. The image twisted his gut. Sydney was tough, he remembered that. She ran track and played basketball in high school and played through half a dozen injuries and not cried once. Pain wasn't a stranger to her so the show of emotion worried him. He looked in her ears for signs of bleeding or hemorrhage behind the eardrum. He flashed a penlight across her pupils and to his relief both reacted equally to light. So far her condition wasn't as dire as it could be, "Where do you hurt, sweetheart?"

"My head and hip."

"EMTs said the car door hit you when the car backed out," he equipped his stethoscope and listened to her lungs and heart. He needed to get the preliminary exam done so he could relieve her pain. "What kind of car do you drive?" That question served two vital purposes. One, it told him the approximate location of probable injuries and two, to test her mental awareness.

"Camaro."

When his fingers pressed into her abdomen, he was pleased with what he felt – or, more to the point, *didn't* feel. At least from his exam, she didn't appear to have internal bleeding, "What year is your Camaro?"

Sydney thought a moment. After a few seconds, she replied, "Ninety-nine."

"Z28 or SS Coupe?"

Sydney didn't answer. Logan watched her brow crease with pain or contemplation or both. Either way, she wasn't responding which concerned him. The answer should have rolled off her tongue. Mentally, he noted the possibility of a concussion. He softly repeated, "Syd, is your car a Z28 or SS Coupe?"

Again there was hesitation but ultimately a reply, "SS Coupe."

"Show-off," he quipped, hoping to drag a smile from her. It worked though pain framed her smile. Gently, he tested her shoulder,

"Did it nail your shoulder too?"

She winced, "Window did."

"Do you remember hitting your head when you fell?"

She barely nodded. Thus far, Logan was satisfied with her condition. He pulled the sheet below her waist to check for noticeable injuries, "I'm not getting fresh, Syd. It's part of the contract you signed when you entered my emergency room."

"Be gentle," she pleaded.

"Now you're hurting my feelings," he joked. "Have I hurt you yet?"

She answered no. He moved across to her pelvis, checked the left side then the right. Sydney bowed on the table, crying, "Not till now. Don't touch me again, Logan."

He cringed. The hip was definitely the problem. Trying to ease her sudden lash of temper, he said completely unruffled, "Normally, I'd be insulted by those words, Syd, but I know you don't mean them."

"At the moment I do."

Jason suddenly appeared again, "Please do something about that ghastly cut on her arm." He shivered, "It hurts me just to look at it."

Logan's vision narrowed. As if he hadn't noticed the three inch slash bleeding through the bandage. He turned to Jason as though he were an interloper, "Mister, who are you and why are you still here after I specifically told you to leave?"

The young man crossed his arms, "I'm Sydney's assistant and I'm here because I'm worried about her."

Ethan's brother firmed his tone while cleaning the blood from the head wound, "Well, Sydney's Assistant, make yourself useful. Call

Ethan, tell him what's happened and tell him not to kill himself driving over here. Now scat."

Jason took wild offense to his tone and huffed his way into her vision, "Honey, I'm being ousted but I'll be right outside if you need me." He cut his vision to Logan, "And I thought Ethan was a brute."

Logan snorted and jerked his head toward the exit, "Out, Assistant."

Through pained eyes, Sydney watched Logan direct the nurse to finish attending to the head wound while he tackled the bleeding arm. She lifted her head somewhat to survey the damage then eased down again, clearly dizzy.

Logan sighed good-naturedly, "Lie down, young lady, and be still. You'll see this later after it's stitched up."

"Can't you just bandage it?"

"No, sweetheart. A bandage won't work but don't worry. I'll try my hand at creative stitching and you might come out with a cute scar."

"Okay." She wormed on the table and instantly regretted it. A loud groan filled the room, "Logan, something for pain. Please."

He nodded to the nurse, "We'll take the edge off for now. Once we find out about your noggin, we might be able to do more. I'm scheduling full x-rays and a CT scan on that pretty head and see if you scrambled anything." Seeing the medication ready, he forewarned her, "Okay, sweetheart, here comes a rush." The nurse slowly injected the medication into the IV. Sydney cringed and Logan patted her arm, "Give it a minute and you'll like me better, I promise. Hopefully, I'll be your every fantasy, your dream come true, your –"

"You're pushing it," she mumbled, then obviously felt a small wave of relief. Taking a deep breath, she sighed, "Then again, maybe you're not."

18

Sydney heard voices from afar. They spiraled toward her in intermittent waves as they had for minutes when they entered the room. She knew the voices – Ethan, Logan and Jason. Logan's was loudest when he cleared his throat annoyingly, "Excuse me, Assistant, why are you trolling your boss's purse?"

Jason, still obviously offended by Logan's presence, replied, "Evidently she has a sister that needs notifying but I cannot find her number, even on Sydney's cell. The brief time she was awake, she mentioned a sister but after that it was back to La La Land."

Sam's fuming would soar to new altitudes when hearing of the accident. Just the mere thought of her tongue-lashing made Sydney's head throb all over again.

Ethan sighed, "Well, hell. I forgot about Samantha." The fact Samantha utterly detested him probably had something to do with his memory loss, Sydney suspected. But then Sam didn't exactly make friends easily, even with family.

He continued, "She lives around Griffin unless she's moved. I'll check the DMV records and get the number."

Through the warped tunnel of drowsiness and medication, she heard Logan dictate, "She's bruised, not broken. Let her know you're here."

Sydney noted as much of the conversation possible but lost some from drifting in and out. The entrance of a new voice, evidently a nurse, brought her back, "Evenin', Dr. Calhoun."

"Evening, Lois. How's our girl?"

"Doing very well. Woke up one time asking for Heath or someone." Sydney felt a blood pressure cuff gradually squeeze down on her arm. *Ethan... His name is Ethan...* Lois spoke again, "Blood pressure's leveling out."

"Let me look at her chart," Logan said. The sharp sound of papers shuffling sliced through her tender brain like knives. Evidently Logan stood beside her while tending to his paperwork. A gentle touch on her forehead, a caress down her cheek and Logan's soft voice brought her awareness to new heights, "Keep her on morphine this evening and if I'm out of the room and her condition changes, page me. I'm still leery of that concussion."

The nurse noted Logan's instructions, "You're off tonight so I'll make a note to call."

"No, I'll be here. I'm staying in case her condition changes."

Ethan's worried voice was next, "What's the problem?"

"She had trouble remembering certain things. Like she couldn't remember if she drove a Z28 or SS Coupe." Following a moment of silence, Sydney detected an almost humorous tone to Logan's voice, "Go say hi to her, *Heath.*"

"Yeah, laugh it up," was all Ethan said. A moment later she heard the reluctance in his voice, "She's so pale."

"Of course she's pale, knucklehead. She was mugged by a car. The door nearly popped her hip apart. I patched her head, and put stitches in her arm. It's the right forearm so be careful. And for God's sake, be careful around that hip."

She floated into light slumber. Unaware of voices and movement, she spiraled deeper until a delicate kiss pressed to her lips. A trembling butterfly kiss. Inching back to wakefulness, she received another kiss to her forehead. A soft, deep tone floated into her ear, "Sydney, baby, it's me."

Slowly her eyes shifted under the lids. The lashes lifted gradually, drowsily. She hoped it was Logan kissing her. Since seeing him hovering above her earlier, Logan recaptured her thoughts and heart with a tremendous passion. A specific lock of black hair ensnared her attention in the ER – the one that fell across his forehead in a particularly sexy way. A lock she wanted to smooth into place then kiss him long and slow. Even racked in agony she wanted that kiss. When she drifted to sleep with the morphine, memories of his soft lips and gentleness lulled her into a restful slumber. "Logan," she whispered.

Silence ensued then a question, "Logan? She thinks I'm you."

Sydney heard a distant low chuckle. It was Logan – an indication he wasn't the one kissing her. Then the eldest answered, "Ethan, give her a break. She's been through a lot today."

She fought to open her eyes. Ethan sounded especially irked that she'd called Logan's name but she couldn't help it. When her vision focused it zeroed in on a holstered gun. The thick, black duty belt spanned a set of strong hips, and she followed them up a burly uniformed chest and ended at a badge. Ethan leaned down until their vision met. Her lips parted in a whisper. Ethan smiled at her, his brown eyes gleamed with emotion as his fingers touched her cheek, "I'm so damn glad to see you're all right."

"Thanks to Logan and Jason," she said voicelessly.

Ethan stroked her hair, his eyes searching her face for more than injuries. She sensed he searched for answers, "I heard. Sugar, you sounded so," he hesitated, "adamant on the phone before you left, like you wanted to say something."

"Ethan, cut it out," Logan admonished. "Interrogating her won't help, plus, it's just out-and-out cruel."

Sydney appreciated his effort however the subject needed tending to. The meeting with Ethan would have to take place right then, despite the fog she drifted in, "Pushkin," she mumbled.

Everyone present heard her. Slowly Logan neared, inadvertently pushing Ethan aside, "Did you say Pushkin, as in the poet?"

Sydney blinked slowly, deliberately, and nodded, trying to remain mentally focused. Ethan's brother noticed Jason nodding too. Her assistant knew about the admirer. Logan bent, his lips so close to her ear she felt his warm breath caress her ear and cheek, "Did you know I like Pushkin too? 'I remember the wonderful moment; Before me you appeared…'"

Sydney's stomach fluttered and even through the cloud of medication, the words penetrated. Her eyes widened slightly as his lips brushed her ear softly, "I'll bet you know that poem by heart." Logan stated it as cold hard fact. Tilting to meet his vision, her response was cut off by Ethan pushing Logan back, "She's my girl so back off. I'll do the whispering from now on."

A brief flash of anger shown in her eyes, surprising them all. The words surfaced sluggish and choppy, "I'm not yours, Ethan. That's what I wanted to say this morning." She saw Jason at the foot of the bed, a tiny smile curving his lips. He gave her a covert thumbs-up, telling her although she slurred most of it, she drove the point home.

Ethan's lungs deflated in a sigh, his shoulders slumped. She feared he might cry the way his lip trembled. His hand took hers and he leaned in, accidentally pressing his weight into her sore hip. She arched painfully on the bed, spurring Logan's temper to erupt, "Damn it, Ethan, you're worse than a bull in a china closet. I told you to be careful with that hip." He grabbed Ethan's shoulders, pushing him toward Jason, "Get him out of here."

Jason drew back at the thought. The imposing sight of Ethan in his uniform caused him to falter until Logan hurled a deadly glare Jason's way. The young man gently took Ethan's arm, "We'll just step outside a moment," he said lightly.

Ethan shook him off, "Syd, it's the drugs making you saying this. We'll talk later. You don't mean it, I realize that."

"Get out, Ethan," Logan ordered. He waited for the door to close then turned back to Sydney, "Still hurting pretty bad?"

Tears welled in her eyes as she nodded, "He didn't mean to."

Reaching into his coat pocket, he withdrew a syringe, "Syd, if anyone knows my brother, it's me. He's naturally clumsy but he's also going to make a scene and upset you." He slipped the needle into the IV,

"Here's a small booster shot. It'll make you sleep a while but you shouldn't hurt as much."

She thanked him, and as he pocketed the syringe, she raised her hand and touched his wrist. He appeared surprised at her touch and covered hers with his free hand, "What is it, sweetheart?"

"I was meeting Ethan to tell him. Ask Jason." She hesitated a moment then, "Please don't hate me. I just don't love Ethan, not the way he loves me."

19

"How could you throw me out like that?" After thirty solid minutes Ethan still breathed fire at his brother. Logan suspected it was more a matter of pride than anything but he doubted Sydney wanted to hold a long discussion about the purpose of hers and Ethan's tragically interrupted meeting.

However Ethan, bless his one-track heart, seethed like no other human could. It positively rankled him not to have his way. Logan sighed then settled back on the bench outside Sydney's room. He occupied his time watching his red-faced, puffed up brother pace the floor, his fists clenched until the flesh blanched lily white.

After seeing Ethan's arms erupt in large, well-defined muscle, Jason backed away – far away into her room – but not before getting visual permission from Logan. The doctor nodded and answered Ethan, "You mashed her for one thing. And secondly, you were pissed off for what she said."

Ethan waved it off, "Morphine makes people loopy. She won't remember what she said."

Don't count on it, he wanted to say. Crossing his ankles, Logan merely cleared his throat. The sound spun Ethan on his heel, "Shut up, Logan."

Surprised at the sudden attack, he recoiled cautiously, "I said nothing."

"Yes, you did. Just without words so shut up."

"You're neurotic and you're right, morphine does affect a person's behavior. But she appears to be very coherent about that subject." Checking his pager, Logan noticed two large feet planted beside his. He followed the legs up to Ethan's red splotched cheeks. Standing to oppose the infuriated expression, Logan tiredly stretched his arms above him, yawning, "You don't want to hear it but you can't keep Syd. Our friend has grown wings and uses them now."

"Yeah, and she flogs me with them every chance she gets. God sakes, I *love* her. Doesn't she know that by now?"

To that, Logan wasn't sure what to say. Sydney did realize Ethan loved her but if Logan affirmed that fact, the knowledge would merely add fuel to a fire that no one could control. Logan was surprised when his brother walked away, the anger melting to quiet defeat. He hated hurting Ethan but after talking to Jason, he learned Sydney had indeed planned to break off Ethan's imagined relationship that morning. He also learned that Pushkin the Admirer had captured her attention to an astonishing degree. Jason gushed about how happy she became since he arrived. Sydney shared more with her assistant than Logan ever imagined. She wondered how Pushkin knew all her favorite flowers, colors and poets. According to Jason, she also caught the hint that she'd eventually remember him.

Hearing Jason speak of Sydney made Logan gain a new appreciation for the young man. He also quickly realized that Jason posed no threat in his pursuit of her. Jason made no bones about his homosexuality and expressed surprise at Sydney's acceptance of his lifestyle.

Logan remarked that that was pure Sydney. She accepted people for themselves and if they didn't betray her or someone she loved, everything was fine with her. That was just one reason why he loved her, he'd nearly said.

Logan stood at the door, peeking through the small crack. Jason sat next to the bed quietly talking on the phone, "What's the bear wearing?"

Logan's brow wrinkled. Now *that* was weird. He listened closer, "A teddy? The bear is wearing a red teddy? How adorable. Have you got a leather skirt instead? All right, the teddy will do. Brighten it up with the leather whip and the bouquet of pink carnations. The card will say something scandalous like, 'Hope this whips you into shape soon. Love Jason.'"

A grin curled Logan's mouth. Knowing Syd, she'd love it. He'd have to grab a present from the gift shop downstairs before nightfall. Probably something without a whip. The carnations weren't a bad idea though.

"Jason can help me. He likes me."
Ethan's voice startled Logan who turned to him asking, "And you believe this why?"

"He treats me pretty well."

"Has nothing to do with the fact you carry a gun, does it? People tend to play nicer if the other person can shoot them."

Ethan scowled at him, "He can change Syd's mind. She's just confused –"

Logan stepped away from the door, his hand urging Ethan to follow, "Do not ask that man to compromise his relationship with Sydney. Not for you."

The anger resurfaced as gnashed teeth and a growl, "You're so pompous when you're not involved. You don't love her, you don't understand."

Logan sucked a deep breath to calm himself but it didn't work. About three years old, he estimated. That was Ethan's current mental age. Sydney obviously emitted a pheromone that impeded and even reversed Ethan's common sense.

The door opened and Jason poked his head out, "Doctor, she's asking for you."

Before Jason finished his sentence, Logan headed inside. Approaching the bed, he lightly touched her hand, "Is something wrong, sweetheart?" He felt her weakly grasp his fingers as her eyelids made a laborious effort to open. Her mouth lifted contentedly, whispering, "I want you, Logan."

His body awakened from toes to ears with the words. The sweet words, uttered like a sleepy child, affected his heart first. The pounding in his chest drowned out Ethan's peeved voice behind him. Logan felt his heart banging painfully against his ribs, the blood coursing in every direction, especially to his groin. A cringe of discomfort later, he swallowed the obvious response and replied, "I'm here, Syd. Do you want me to stay?"

"Please," her lips moved slowly, lethargically and she nodded off again.

Amidst the thundering in his chest a familiar pain registered there. The feeling from many years ago. Love. Had she said it or had he just hoped? His greatest fear was that Ethan was right. That the morphine played tricks with her mind and she only *thought* she wanted Logan.

"Why is she wanting *you?*" Ethan nearly shouted.

Logan pressed a soft kiss to her forehead then stood, "Ethan, if you can't keep your voice down, leave. Behave for once in your life."

Ethan bulled his way to him, pushing Jason sideways to clear the path, "No, damn it. You're going to tell me what's going on between you two."

Having had enough, Logan palmed the phone and pushed a button, "Good Lord, *nothing* is going on between us. You're getting ridiculous about this situation. Until you screw your head on right, get out."

Stunned at Logan's drastic order, Ethan grabbed his arm, his voice wavering between anger and desperation, "I'm your brother, Logan and Sydney's my –"

"Sydney's *my* patient. When you can control yourself, you'll be allowed in. Until then," he pointed to the door.

Ethan shot him a glare that withered Jason from five feet away.

"Fine," the younger brother growled. "Here's Sam's phone

number. You get the privilege of calling her."

Logan calmly plucked it from his trembling hand and watched him stalk out. He stared at the Griffin phone number knowing Samantha Eatonton would not be pleasant to deal with, especially when she realized it was him. They hadn't exactly parted friends since she threatened to call the police for harassment. After Sydney left town, he approached Samantha asking Sydney's whereabouts, literally begging Sam for answers. She hadn't yielded an inch and after four more visits, Sam refused to let him in. Ignoring her, he stormed in, his hands firmly seizing her shoulders and insisted on the information. Admittedly, he backed her into a corner, looming over her until Sam shoved him backwards with the threat to notify the police.

A quiet voice emerged from a corner, "I'll call, if you'd like."

Logan sighed with relief, "Thank you, Jason. I think Samantha would appreciate hearing from someone other than a Calhoun."

20

Samantha Eatonton marched briskly down the halls of Atlanta Medical, a woman determined and on a mission. Her long, dark waves bounced with each step, her lips pursed as she noted the time on her watch. It seemed longer than three hours since Jason Butler called her but thanks to traffic snarls and dodging accidents, it really had taken two hours to travel the thirty-nine miles from Griffin – all while worrying about Sydney.

Sam knew something like this would eventually happen. Atlanta wasn't safe. That's why she moved to Griffin ten years ago. Finding out Sydney's promotion brought her back to the city inspired many sleepless nights for Samantha. Mothering – as Sydney labeled it – came naturally. Being the eldest held a certain amount of responsibility, especially when Sydney never took things seriously enough. Now she was in the hospital because some moron hit her while stealing her car. That damned Camaro. Sam shook her head again. For some reason, Sydney cherished the red beast from the time she bought it. Before Sydney's move, Sam begged her to trade cars for something less high profile with thieves. No, she kept the car, moved to Atlanta and now Sam walked the halls of Atlanta Medical Center searching for her hospital room.

After learning Sydney's room was located on the second floor, Sam replayed the information Sydney's assistant gave her. A possible hairline fracture in the right hip, stitches in the right arm and a slight concussion. It riled Sam that a physician took such a casual attitude about her sister's condition. She never believed in "slight" concussions. Being hit by a car caused massive internal damage, broken bones and life-threatening concussions. Her little sister probably clung to one thread of life and Samantha intended to take charge while nursing Sydney back to health – whether the kid liked it or not.

The black stiletto heels echoed through the hall with a determined cadence. Navigating the ice and snow with spike heels made her feel akin to a comedic act, either sliding hither and yon or having the spikes trench deep into the ice. But she hadn't taken time to change because the call came at work – well, technically at home but she checked her messages frequently through the day. When a nervous male voice announced her sister had been in an accident and to call back on Sydney's cell number, Sam did just that. That was her first encounter with Jason Butler. A seemingly friendly, open man that cared tremendously about her sister. Sam could be partial to a man like him.

She stopped at the nurse's station, "Sydney Eatonton's room, please, and her doctor's name also."

Without looking up, the nurse flipped through a stack of charts, "Room 214 and Dr. Logan Calhoun is the attending physician."

Sam blinked. Perching her slim hands on the counter, she leaned closer, unsure of what she heard. Logan? A doctor? *Sydney's* doctor? The day couldn't possibly have slid *that* far downhill, could it? "I'm sorry. Did you say Logan Calhoun?"

"Yes, ma'am," the nurse concurred.

Obviously, the day could slide *that* far down. As far as Sam was concerned it plummeted all the way to the bowels of hell.

Her eyes and lips narrowed. She remembered Logan too well. Just as Sydney and Ethan shared the same grade, so had she and Logan. Sam recalled the day Sydney ran home from school asking why a boy would stick his tongue in her mouth. Without explaining to the sixth grader, Sam merely asked if Ethan did it. With wide, innocent eyes, her sister blushed, answering no, Logan had. Thus began Sam's earnest dislike for the older Calhoun. She'd bawled him out before algebra class, warning him to find girls his own age. Logan, amused at her lecture, had laughed at her. Actually *laughed* at her. Shortly after gaining his composure, a wicked gleam flashed in his brown eyes and he drew her to him by the waist. He planted his lips squarely on hers before giving her time to object. She'd shoved away from him, her temper rising at his brazen behavior and at his arrogance that she might fawn over his kiss as Sydney had. Logan dug himself deeper with Sam by winking, "You're tempting but I think I'll stick with Syd."

Frustrating and assuming, that's how Sam remembered Logan. Age, she guessed, would only root those particular qualities deeper – so deep she'd probably pull him inside out if she tried to remove them so she braced herself for an impending battle.

Approaching her sister's room, she noticed a lean young man in his mid-twenties slumped on a bench. Fatigue wore heavy in his expression when he glanced up at the closed door. Sydney's purse sat beside him, propped against his hip. As she neared, she noticed his hand went protectively to it. She cleared her throat, "Excuse me."

The man ran a hand through his sandy blond hair and sighed. Lifting his gaze, he met her stern expression, "Yes?"

"I'm Samantha Eatonton. Are you Jason Butler?"

Jason's weary vision widened as he rose to stand. This was Sydney's sister? Now *this* was the definition of dominatrix. A short black skirt hugged her firm thighs and a white satin blouse clung to her tall, trim form and a black designer jacket was slung over her arm. From her presence, Jason noticed Samantha not only sported a more unyielding attitude than Sydney but was also blessed with the lion's share of endowment. The sisters favored in some ways however. Both were gifted with natural beauty, Sydney's being softer than Sam's and both sisters possessed captivating eyes. To Jason, Sam's blue eyes pierced rather than caressed, like Sydney's green ones. And the determined slant of her jaw reminded him of the younger Eatonton, but only when Sydney was ticked off. It was that killer look. Literally, killer – Sam owned it and used it. He eased his hand out with a measurable degree of apprehension, "Yes... Yes, I'm Jason Butler."

With no trace of a smile, Samantha grasped his hand firmly, giving it a good shake, "Thank you for calling me. How is she?"

"In and out of consciousness all day. Evidently the doctor is giving her morphine so that explains part of it."

"You mean Logan?"

She grumbled the words, giving Jason the distinct feeling he'd stepped in an enormous, stinky pile of poo. In Samantha's world, "Logan" was a dirty word and he'd definitely remember that henceforth. He decided retreating backward a step was the best option as he nodded.

"Is he in there now?"

Jason forced another nod and Sam finished, "Good. I can tell him now."

"Tell him what?"

"That he's being replaced as Sydney's physician." Readjusting the shoulder strap of her purse, she pointed to the open handbag next to Jason's hip, "That belongs to my sister, I assume?"

Skewered by the needling glare, he quickly gathered it up while nodding, "I only looked through it to find your number." The hand reaching out, he noted, exhibited perfectly manicured fingernails. The sight sent a shiver through him. A man could be impaled on such talons and he knew Samantha Eatonton sported plenty of notches on her belt.

From first glance, Sydney and Samantha were polar opposites. Sydney was refreshing, friendly, and earthy with a playful sense of humor. Samantha, while as gorgeous as her younger sibling, appeared cold, indifferent and, well, quite frankly, bitchy. Behind the dark blue eyes, Jason sensed a manipulative female who forced everyone around her to conform or face dire consequences. No wonder, Jason thought, her left hand had no ring on it and for the first time in years, he felt grateful he was gay.

Surprisingly, Samantha's pursed lips lifted to smile, "I appreciate you calling me. No one else would have."

"Well," Jason volunteered timidly, "it was Ethan who ultimately located your number."

Just the mere mention of Ethan's name steeled her again and Jason regretted opening his silly mouth. Both brothers were taboo from now on. Let someone else receive the nasty, heated glares. Enduring another convinced Jason he'd melt into the floor.

Samantha peered through narrowed eyes, "*He's* not here, is he?"

This time he shook his head, knowing the news pleased Sam. He wanted to please her if, for nothing else, to stop the glare she insisted on frying him with.

Thankfully, her expression seemed to relax with the information, "At least they're not swarming her yet. Thanks again for calling me, Mr. Butler. You may go home now."

Jason stammered again, his brow puckering, his tone wounded, "But...but I'd like to see how she does this evening."

She rifled her purse, retrieved a pen and paper, "Leave your number and I'll call you. There's really no need for you to stay since I'm here now."

Jason's frown deepened. Who was this woman to order him home? Did she honestly think she could manipulate him too? He may have been gay but never spineless.

Taking the pen and paper, he scribbled his name and number, "Until she's settled for the evening, I'm staying. You can call me tomorrow if anything changes."

Jason's fortitude disrupted her train of thought. Sam stared at him momentarily, sizing him up then capitulated, "She'll be glad you stayed. And I'll call you with an update tomorrow." She tucked the information into her purse, faced the door, and blew out a breath. Confronting Logan after so many years was like having a root canal without Novocain.

She recalled the last time she saw him. She remembered his large form blocking the entry after he'd shouldered the wooden door open. His strong hands grasped her shoulders and his body shook with rage when he demanded to know where her sister was. For the first time in her life, she experienced utter panic around Logan Calhoun. With every rejection she expressed, his fury intensified to the point he backed Sam to the wall. She could still feel his thumbs pressing into her collarbones and fingertips digging into her shoulder blades as he towered over her. He hadn't hurt her but the hold soundly prevented her from fleeing his barrage of questions.

He wanted Sydney and Sam blockaded his way by keeping quiet. That's what frightened Samantha the most. Logan craved her sister with an appetite that alarmed her. Sam wasn't stupid. She knew physical force was no stranger in the Calhoun house and Logan, without intending to, might hurt Sydney – that was her fear at the time. Samantha refused to allow it, even if she took a wallop herself in the process.

Shoving the memories aside, she took a deep breath and pushed the door open. The first image greeting her was a well-built, broad-shouldered man with coal black hair sitting in a window alcove, his back braced against the wall, asleep. He wore a dark blue button down shirt tucked into his well worn jeans. Those jeans encased thick, muscular legs that folded knees to chest in the tiny alcove. He resembled a little boy with his wavy hair askew across his forehead. Then recognition dawned. Logan.

She tried to tip-toe to Sydney's side but the heels didn't lend themselves to stealthy movement. Suddenly she heard Logan grunt. She turned to see his head jerk backward as he suddenly awakened and his noggin thumped the wall as a result. He cursed under his breath while rubbing the back of his head.

The moment their vision met, Sam felt something from him. The feeling wasn't entirely new. A lot of men expressed the look around her: cautious interest. But Logan tossed in another emotion, temporarily throwing her. His eyes flashed a specific warning that she read as a protective measure. Logan finally had Sydney in his presence and wasn't allowing *anyone* to threaten it, especially Sam.

The urge to break eye contact overwhelmed her. His cold resentment assailed her far more brutally than the Arctic air blowing outside. She watched as his long legs straightened, the large feet planted squarely on the floor. Logan stretched, his arms reaching skyward, his fingers splaying wide. Sam's stomach twisted. Was he always this menacingly tall? Even as he approached, the imminent urge to escape swelled inside but she couldn't leave Sydney alone. Not with him.

His hand extended and a deep, soothing voice greeted her, "Hello, Samantha."

Seeing him reach for her, Sam took a hesitant step back. He didn't sound as hostile as he looked, thankfully. She placed her hand in his. His warm fingers closed, nearly enveloping her entire hand and tenderly squeezed, "You look good, Sam. How've you been?"

"I've been better," she replied honestly. "Since she moved back to Atlanta I've lost a year's worth of sleep worrying something like this might happen." Retrieving her hand, she turned to see Sydney resting peacefully, her breathing slow and even. "She's so bull-headed..."

"Like her sister," Logan added.

Sam swiveled back to him, intent on following up with a reference to the past. Logan cut her thoughts short, "She's doing well for what she's been through. I'm keeping her overnight for a few reasons, one being the slight concussion..."

"*Slight?*" she croaked. Her arms folded, her distant and cold attitude returning, "How can a person be hit by a car and have a *slight* concussion, Logan? Here's what I want done to ensure she's okay..." She proceeded to rattle off a battery of tests, instructing him why they should be done and when, concluding, "Because surely you do *not* expect me to take only *your* word concerning her condition."

Logan clenched his jaw, his glare sharpened. The longer her list grew the more irritated he clearly became, narrowing his brown eyes until they darkened nearly black, "Exactly what is it with you Eatonton dames? Neither of you trust my expertise. She thought I was going to kill her when they brought her in and now you..." he shoved a hand through his unruly hair, combing it back. "Maddening, that's what you two are."

Now this was the Logan she remembered. Arrogant and

obstinate. The intensity of his complaint stopped her. Logan shifted closer which caused her to move back as he explained, "She's had a CT scan and x-rays. She doesn't need all the other tests. It would waste time, money and it would, no doubt, piss her off."

Samantha planted her small feet, determined to have her say, determined to win, "Being pissed off is better than being dead. You'll do these tests or else."

Logan moved forward pushing her closer to the wall, "Or else what? You want a second opinion, fine, but I'm not putting Syd through all that for nothing."

"Well," punctuating her intent, she poked a finger into Logan's chest, "*Doctor* Calhoun, I want more than a second opinion. I want all of Sydney's records and treatment handled by another physician."

Logan bristled. His wide shoulders formed a menacing blockade between her and the door. He focused on the finger threatening to stab him again and it did, causing him to flinch. *Good*, she thought. And just in case he misunderstood, "I want it done within the hour."

Logan captured the delicate finger like a bothersome fly, "I won't release her to anyone else because she's *my* patient."

Samantha stared up into his fiery expression. If he thought dumping a load of testosterone into the equation would help his cause, he sorely underestimated her. She tugged her finger free of Logan's grasp and upped the ante, smiling, "Oh, I think a visit to the hospital's director will change your mind."

Logan's dark eyes flashed with ire and his fists went to his hips, "Want to share a room with your sister?"

Stunned by not only his bluntness but also his calm delivery of the threat, she stammered, "You... you wouldn't dare."

Logan restrained his temper long enough to level a fierce scowl at Sam, "Try me. I take my oath seriously, despite what you think. Syd is sore as hell but she'll recover. *Trust me.*"

A condescending laugh filled the room. Across the small room, Sydney stirred slightly. Logan watched her, hoping the noise didn't wake her. Thankfully, her eyes remained closed. Samantha lowered her voice, "Trust a Calhoun. After what Ethan did to her, *there's no way.* Your participation is a conflict of interest, Logan, you should realize that. I'm supposed to feel warm and fuzzy knowing a man that wanted to sleep with her is her physician? You're looking at her, touching her and you're able to retain an objective –"

"That's enough," Logan said, hoping to end the quarrel before it escalated yet again. He knew her temper flared from old, ugly memories but her relentless attitude grated on his nerves.

"What's wrong? The truth difficult to accept?"

Electing to ignore her ranting, Logan instead chose to exercise his power, "I've banned Ethan from seeing her, I can do the same with you."

The warning spiked her anger. Samantha bolted from the corner, her jaw set, "Don't you threaten me, Logan. Sydney's *my sister* and you can't do that."

His large hands braced her shoulders, stopping her, "You have no choice. I have the authority here so if you don't keep your voice down and," he lowered his tone, "your mouth shut, I will prohibit you from seeing her."

Even with her heels, he towered over her. Looking up, she pursed her lips then muttered, "You pick a hell of a time for payback."

"This isn't payback. She needs rest and our arguing won't help her recuperate."

"You could prevent this by transferring her records to another physician."

Logan thrust his fists in his jeans as a preventative measure. His hands itched to shake her silly. His tone confirmed it, "Why do you always act like this? Ever since junior high you've acted like I'm a friggin' serial rapist. Sydney's the *only* woman I've ever wanted…"

Samantha watched his hands race from his pockets and the palms smack his forehead. Under his breath, he cursed himself as his hand slid down his cheek and scrubbed his jaw. His fatigued vision trained on Sydney and Sam practically heard his prayer that her sister hadn't overheard the revelation.

Samantha stood, appalled and mute. As though the clouds finally parted to allow a harsh truth to filter into her brain, her wide blue eyes lifted to his dark ones.

Logan's vision cautiously met hers, "Listen, Sam –"

"You're serious," she declared, astonished. Reaching behind her for a chair, the irony of situation struck her hard. Logan wanted Sydney and Sydney wanted Logan and neither of them knew it. He slid a chair under her as she stared at her sister, the chaste bewilderment seizing control of her thoughts.

Sam knew for the past several years Sydney loved him – without Sydney actually saying so. Her actions spoke louder than words. The inability to be happy unless talking about Logan and wondering about him then verbally retreating with the excuse he'd never forgive her for the past. Instead, Sydney settled for men like Ethan or Travis Shaw and Sam knew it was some bizarre punishment for rejecting Logan years ago. "This is unbelievable," she mumbled. "And you love her?"

"Of course I do," he stated in obvious defeat. Leaning against the wall, he sighed, "Ever since high school I've loved her but she always went to Ethan and I wasn't going to fight my brother in a losing battle."

"Is that why you French-kissed her in sixth grade?" She noticed he cringed at the mention of the kiss.

"Will I ever live that down?" he mumbled under his breath.

"Doubtful," she answered, a slight smile curving her lips. "Though she said you're pretty good at it."

His head lifted with a hopeful – but still wary expression, "Why aren't you throwing a shoe at my Freudian slip?"

Shaking her head, an exasperated smirk crossed her face, "I'm not throwing a shoe because, one, I'm physically and mentally exhausted, two, I'm sick of dancing this dance with you, and three, my sister deserves happiness."

"You make it sound like I have a chance. Last account I had, she ran away from me in tears."

"Oh, grow up, Logan. She'd just seen her fiance, your brother, screwing another woman. So you chose the wrong time to approach her. Try again. Last account *I* had, you were as stubborn as she is." She refused to tell him how Sydney pined for him. Sam figured with little encouragement, Logan would make his move and this time, Sydney would gleefully say yes. She'd let the two work it out without any interference from her.

"No offense, Samantha, but I expected a tremendous battle with you."

"No offense taken. Sydney isn't a child, she can make her own decisions now. Yes, I protected her because Ethan hurt her and I put you in the same category. Can you blame me? You both came 'round like clockwork, always frustrated, if you know what I mean," he pointed to his crotch. "I wasn't turning either of you loose on her, not like that."

"I wouldn't have hurt her. I just wanted another chance with her."

"At the time I interpreted your actions differently. But I believe if you still love her, you should try again. She hasn't been happy since she left Atlanta." *And you.*

His hand extended again and this time she took it easily, pleased with the last half hour's events. Maybe Sydney would find happiness – finally.

"Sam," he whispered.

Her vision rose to his. Logan pressed a kiss to her knuckles, smiling a sexy grin, "Thanks."

She barely curbed her own smile, "Don't try to charm me, Logan

Calhoun. I've seen that smile work on other women but I'm immune."

He toned down the potency, "Having your support means a lot to me."

Her smile ebbed to a hesitant one, "Just don't hurt her. She's had enough pain in her life."

Sydney heard voices. They longer they spoke the closer to consciousness she drifted until her eyes gradually opened. Logan and Sam entered her bleary vision. Sam kissed her cheek, "How long have you been awake?"

"Just now," was the thick reply. "My leg feels like something's eating it."

Sam's worried expression faced Logan who eased her concern with a nod, "You've got some nerve damage from the hip injury. You'll have it a while." He rounded the right side, waving Samantha over.

Sydney's eyes followed his hands and the moment they reached for the blanket, she stopped him. Logan's brow sank, "Syd, don't. Samantha needs to see your arm and your side."

She shook her head. He grasped the covers only for her to sluggishly battle him. Logan fought both persistent hands and their lethargic, flimsy shoving and finally sighed, "Young lady, stop this immediately."

His sharp, deep tone halted her. "Stop calling me that," was her hoarse reply. The effort it took to complete a sentence didn't seem worth it. It completely exhausted her. Why did Logan insist on doing this? Seeing the wounds would only fuel Samantha's tirades about the Camaro again and frankly she'd heard enough.

"Then stop acting like a child, Sydney. I assume you'll go home with Sam so she needs to know your injuries and how to care for them."

Sydney's lips parted again but nothing emerged. In her morphine fog, she completely forgot about her job, much less the ramifications the accident caused regarding it. Griffin was forty miles from Atlanta and driving that every day not only would wear Sam out but jeopardize her job as well. Only problem was Sydney used her vacation to move from Savannah so she *had* to stay at her apartment or risk losing her employment status. That thought alone caused her aching head to revive its tribal rhythm. The hospital and doctor bills, not to mention replacing her car and dealing with all the insurance companies... The reality of her situation didn't trickle into her mind, it poured. Through clouded vision and thick tongued words, she vowed, "I'll be fine at home."
Logan laughed and not to Sydney's amusement either. She frowned at his cheerful features, "Something funny?"

"Yes, sweetheart. Your notions are comical at best." Then the smile gave way to stony seriousness, "And fatal at worst. Ethan told me where you're living. Even healthy you're taking a risk. In this shape you're doomed. Lose the pride, Syd, it's not becoming." Logan pushed the covers back, "Now behave."

The instant Samantha laid eyes on the massive dark purple bruise and stitched arm, she groaned. Judging from her sister's wide-eyed stare, the injuries were as obvious as if Elvis entered the room.

She hadn't looked at herself but she could feel. Oh Lord, could she feel... She also felt Sam's lecture growing by the minute.

Purposefully ignoring Logan's repertoire of her body's damage, she laid still, seething through the cloud of medication. Then Sydney's sleepy green eyes flashed with muted temper, and a lacking, almost humorous temper fit arose. She aimed her ire at Logan, "You're making things worse. If you'd only...," Her voice trailed to nothing. The stormy air enveloping his mood halted her words, stole her thoughts.

Logan's dark eyes turned coal black. Any hint of good humor evaporated, "Listen carefully, *young lady*. I'll speak slowly so the words will penetrate your scrambled brain." Bending closer until he got a clear view of her bewildered, pale eyes, he followed up with, "You will require assistance showering, changing your clothes, and walking, insignificant tasks like that." Then an idea hit him. The longer he mulled it over, the wider his grin spread. His mama always said even a hog could find an acorn once in a while. If so, this was a hell of an acorn. Logan never felt more like a lottery winner than right then.

Sydney's brow drew downward, "Why are you grinning like that?"

From the corner of his vision he noticed Sam leaning in to survey the situation as well, "You do seem to have feathers hanging out of your mouth. What's going on?"

He spoke to Sam without breaking eye contact with her sister, "I'm offering Syd a choice. She can go home with you or with me."

He'd heard Samantha gasp at the offer of taking Sydney home with him. He wasn't wasting time making his move. Admirer or not,

Sydney would go home with him and he'd reveal his identity to her. The advantages of staying with Logan outweighed traveling the many miles to Griffin. He was a doctor, his place was closer to Fantasy than Sydney's apartment, and he could help her shower and dress. The last part made his gut tighten. He reminded himself to focus on the goal at hand, not lose himself in the daydreams flitting through his imagination.

Sydney's eyes widened a bit as he pinned her with his stare. Her vision lowered to his mouth, a provocative move, non-threatening to her but it aroused the hell out of him. He couldn't resist it any longer. He leaned in and brushed her lips with his. He assumed she'd be surprised by the bold move. Instead, her eyes closed with the contact and, God help him, he swore she responded to the brief touch.

Her lips remained slightly puckered – evidently awaiting another kiss so he happily obliged. He pressed his lips to hers, slowly this time.

He felt her respond tenderly as her eyes slowly opened then leisurely closed again. He smiled against her lips, prompting her to look at him, the pupils engulfing her green irises. She liked the kiss, liked his nearness. When he pulled back, she gifted him with her answer, "I'll go with you."

"There's my girl. I promise you won't regret it."

Sydney addressed her sister, "No comments?"

"Besides 'that's a hell of a way to take someone's temperature', no. It's your life, Syd. Just make sure it's what you want. I still retain visitation rights during your convalescence, though."

Logan nodded, "You'll have my address before Syd's release."

Straightening, he gently probed around the bruised hip, judging the area by touch. Occasionally she winced and angled away slightly.

He checked another area, "Be still. Also be warned if you misbehave, there are all manner of unpleasant tests I will schedule for you." He winced sympathetically as she cringed.

He hit a horribly sore spot and Sydney blurted, "Oh, you can be thoroughly hateful. If I go with you, you'd better promise not to touch me."

The latter statement lacked the vehemence of the first. In fact, he detected a dare in the tone. Logan shook his head, "I don't think so. I get such little joy from this job anyway so when I have you all to myself, I think I'll make it my new hobby to touch you. Banning me from my new hobby would take all the fun out of life."

"That's me, the party-pooper."

He blinked with a sudden thought, "Say, how *is* your bowel system? Are you regular?"

Her vision noticeably sharpened, honed to the point of shooting daggers, "Leave my bowels alone, Logan. They're just fine."

He laughed again, "Then it's a good thing I didn't listen to your sister."

She looked at Samantha who simply blushed sheepishly while addressing Logan, "You haven't changed a bit. Always getting me into trouble."

He couldn't resist, "According to Sam, you needed tests on your upper and lower GI. To rule out internal injuries, so she said."

Sydney frowned at her sister, "No, she just evidently hates me."

Sam sighed, "I had good intentions. But," she drawled heavily,

"*Doctor Calhoun* set me on the straight and narrow."

"He set *you* straight?" she gaped. The longer she was awake, the stronger her voice became and more coherent her words sounded. Even the shock of his verbal victory over Samantha seemed to register.

Logan's hand drifted lower on her stomach and she slapped again, only this time he caught her wrist firmly and held. Sydney's vision lifted to his. He informed, "I have restraints, young lady. Don't think I won't use them. I just assumed you weren't interested in being tied down unless it's in the privacy of a bedroom."

Bingo, Logan thought. The blush crept up past her ears. Her response would be interesting because her body's reaction certainly was. His grip tightened slightly as she attempted to tug free, "You wouldn't..."

"Don't dare this man today, Syd," Samantha warned. "I have a feeling you'll lose."

He nodded, "Sam is a wise woman." While holding Sydney's left hand, he began the exam again. When he gently pressed, she whimpered, struggling to escape his torment but his hold kept her immobile, "You can stop any time, Dr. Marquis De Sade."

He continued probing gently, concentrating on what he felt, "Syd, I'm not hurting you on purpose."

The strength in her voice returned full force but she didn't push his hand away. She'd obviously been lectured enough, "Well, if you go any lower you need a different medical degree to examine me."

"Spoilsport," he retorted, pleased she felt good enough to spar with him.

21

Samantha programmed Sydney's cell phone, her words unmistakably stern, "Why wasn't my number in your cell?"

Sydney wondered why she'd awakened at that particular time. She'd had enough, she thought, now she had to placate her mulish sister. Sydney knew the damn phone number by heart but never got around to plugging it in her phone.

"Never got the new number programmed," Sydney's throaty voice replied. "Sorry." What she assumed to be a harmless response only fueled Sam's discord. Holding the phone in one hand, Sam purposefully stabbed each number with her thumb, "I've had this number for six months. It should be in here and now it is." Temporarily, she directed her whole attention at her sister, "You scared the hell out of me." She tore a tissue from the pink Kleenex box sitting on the cabinet and dabbed the corners of her eyes, "You're the only sister I have. When I heard what happened..."

Sydney reached for her hand and held it, "I'm okay, Samantha. Calm down."

"Calm down she says," she sputtered. "You didn't have to call Mother and Daddy. Try explaining to a couple halfway around the world that their youngest child nearly died *and* that Logan Calhoun was the attending physician."

Oh... "I suppose they were especially unhappy about that last part."

"The goddess of understatement. Daddy actually called the hospital to check Logan's credentials. They're calling you this afternoon so be ready. I haven't told them you're going home with him. I thought I'd suffered enough." Sam wadded the tissue in her fist and cautiously approached the subject, "So how *do* you feel about going with Logan?"

Sydney's impish grin prompted Sam to chuckle, "That's what I thought."

"You seemed to get along pretty well. What happened?"

"Age, honey. We all learn what's important the older we get and saving your life raised his merit with me." Samantha's tone alerted her sister not to push the conversation.

The door opened prompting Sydney to turn toward it. She hoped it might be another bear. The one Jason sent amused Logan, worried Sam and intrigued Sydney. The little brown bear stood about a foot tall and wore a red lace teddy. Fire red lipstick painted its tiny puckered lips as it winked suggestively to its new owner – or as suggestively as a garishly dressed bear could wink. Logan especially liked the nine inch black leather whip in the bear's paw, "Step out of line again, young lady, and I'll use this," he'd said. She spent the better part of the morning twirling the small lash around her fingers and swinging it back and forth in her hand. That, along with Logan's flower arrangement of pink carnations, purple iris and burgundy roses made her feel like royalty. He'd signed the card "With much love, Logan". She hadn't allowed herself to get too attached to the word love. Men said it but sometimes meant it different ways.

The man walking in this morning wasn't a delivery man at all. It was Ethan dressed in his lieutenant's uniform, his wavy hair askew and his jaw shadowed with overnight growth.

Samantha prickled immediately, "Logan prohibited you from seeing her. I'll get security if you don't leave."

"Chill, woman. I came here for a couple of reasons, one to see how Syd was doing."

"I'm fine, Ethan. Logan's taking excellent care of me."

"I'll just bet," he deadpanned.

Samantha faced him in a most mismatched confrontation. Even wearing heels, she stood five inches shorter than he, her build frail in comparison. With one good huff or puff, he could have bowled her over but she stood her ground, protecting Sydney as always, "Don't cause trouble, Ethan. She's doing okay but if you upset her, I will tell Logan."

"Wow. I'm shaking, Sam," he displayed his large hands: they remained completely steady. He wrapped his hands around her shoulders and moved her aside. Sam fought against him, "Release me now or I'll call your superiors and tell them about their rogue officer. I will make your life miserable if you hurt Sydney or me."

His vision lowered to hers and Sydney swore her sister froze instantly. The voice that emerged didn't sound like Ethan. It sounded leaden with molten rage, "You got it wrong. Your sister is the one hurting people, not me. I wanted to inform her we found her car on Riverside Drive." He turned to Sydney, "Call your insurance company. It was stripped and totaled. Tell 'em it's in the DeKalb County impound. I had what's left of it towed there."

Sydney swallowed hard and nodded, "Thank you, Ethan." In her life, she hadn't seen Ethan so cold, not to her. His presence sent a bitter chill through her, making her shudder. The motion wracked her right side with new waves of raw pain and she bit her lip, cringing.

"Well," his thumb hitched indifferently toward his badge, "I'm here to serve so I'm serving you." He scrubbed his hand along his stubbled jaw, gathering his courage, "Still on morphine?"

She shook her head timidly. He nodded once in response, "Good. Still want Logan?"

Sam's jaw dropped at his blatant manner. Ethan's black eyes pierced her, apparently sensing her confusion, "She kept asking for him yesterday, not me. She didn't ask for the man who loved her and wanted to protect her –"

"Ethan, please –" Sydney began only to have Sam raise a hand, silencing her. The eldest Eatonton took over, "I'm calling security. You can leave or be forcibly removed. This isn't the time or place to discuss this." She stepped past him toward the phone. His hand grasped her elbow hard enough she recoiled in pain, "When's the proper time and place, Miss Manners? After my brother's bedded and wedded her?"

Gasping at his outrageous behavior, she tensed, ready to do battle. Then to everyone's relief – except Ethan's – the door opened again and Logan walked in. Upon seeing Sam's infuriated expression, he announced, "Your face will freeze like that. Didn't your mother tell you?" Then he caught sight of Ethan and groaned.

Sydney swallowed hard. Apart from her, no one saw Ethan's hand roll into a fist and the muscles in his jaws tighten. If Logan noticed, he chose not to acknowledge it. The uniformed time bomb finally spoke through clenched teeth, "Nice to see you too, brother."

Tiredly rubbing the back of his neck, Logan prepared for another round with his brother, "Ethan, I told you, you can't come in."

Sam's chin tilted up, looking straight into Ethan's angered features, "He was just leaving."

"Good," Logan replied, "then you'll release Samantha's arm before she files charges. By the looks of your hold, she may have bruises as proof of your brutality. Go home and calm down." He held the door for his brother who freed Sam from his hold. Swiveling on one foot to Sydney, his grim expression darkened, "You'll need me one day. When you do, you'll beg for my help."

Logan put a hand to Ethan's shoulder, "Go home."

The youngest Calhoun angrily swung away from the touch, "You'll regret this, Logan. Mark my words." He punctuated his declaration by stalking out and slamming the door behind him.

22

When they stepped inside Logan's house, Sydney gained a new respect for the elder Calhoun. The quaint little one-story located in a historic neighborhood sat nestled comfortably in a cluster of oaks and maples. Sydney could only imagine the beauty in Fall. The little brick house trimmed in buff appeared to have been painted in the last year or so.

"It's not much," Logan had said, "and it still needs a lot of work. I bought it as a fixer-upper with hopes I'd have some time to renovate. It's slow but steady. I've repainted, re-carpeted and renovated the living room and bedroom."

He'd gone on about his plans for the place, how he wanted to restructure the garden along the walkway, that he planned to knock out a wall between two bedrooms and make a larger master bedroom and bath.

Although the house sat back from the street, it still projected a uniqueness among the two-story larger homes surrounding it.

An emerald carpet of Zoysia grass led to arched French doors. He pointed to the flower bed, "My neighbor helps me with this. She recommended caladiums for the pots over here," he pointed to two large concrete urns framing the sidewalk.

Sydney couldn't help the pang of jealousy winding through her. Another woman helping Logan plan his flower beds. *Oh, for Pete's sake,* she admonished herself, *he's not your husband. Get over it...*

Somehow detecting her resentment, Logan eased his arm around her shoulders, "Mrs. Davidson is seventy-three. She's a member of the Garden Club of Georgia so I suspect she knows her flowers."

Nice, Syd. Now you look like a moron. "I suspect you're right," she eked out sheepishly.

Stepping inside, she noticed Logan's tension escalated. Why she didn't know, unless it was the need of a woman's opinion. Once the light switched on, Sydney discovered Logan had many talents, decorating being high on the list. The room radiated comfort yet a masculine air. Large maple stained ceiling beams framed ivory painted walls, giving the room a rustic feel. Muted light glowed from recessed lights in the beams, producing a warm ambiance. Sydney's vision traveled from those to the cream brick fireplace with arched opening. Off to each side sat copper colored accent chairs, each with an ottoman. The fabric looked velvet soft, inviting her to try them. Across from the chairs was a couch with the same color fabric. Standing on either side were potted ferns. "Are you sure you're not married?" she'd asked him.

Logan had laughed but a man with this style was, quite frankly, scary. He told her he'd done the decorating himself but this rivaled a professional's job and it flushed Ethan's beer-bottles-make-great-accents taste, no question.

Adorning the living room walls were prints of Cezanne, Pissarro and Degas. The Degas print of a woman's nude profile, sitting and toweling her long dark hair intrigued her. She pointed, "That's an interesting print."

He shrugged, "Reminded me of you. Couldn't resist."

Sydney wasn't sure whether he was serious or not. By his expression, yes, he was.

He escorted her to the bedroom, pronouncing it hers until she tired of it. She practically choked. She'd never tire of an exquisite room. Hunter green curtains accented textured cream colored walls. Under her feet was the softest, thickest hunter carpet she'd ever felt. Before entering the room, he flipped on the mood lighting above the headboard, and she gained another respect for Logan. Logan the Lover. Flanking each side of the headboard like sentries, two open top lanterns hung on the wall, cylindrical in shape with amber globes trimmed in dark copper. A dark copper ceiling fan hung overhead, its oak blades turning slowly and silently above the bed.

She sat down, testing the bed carefully. Settling her weight mostly on her left hip she noted the mattress felt just right. She took the time to admire the heavy four poster bed. With the dark green sheets, the king size bed should have swallowed half the room but it didn't. That, along with the matching nightstand and five drawer chest combined to make the room cozy. The room smelled like Logan. A fine mixture of spice and male scent mingled in the air. Hormones be damned, she wanted Logan Calhoun. By the look on his face, he felt the same way about her but he'd forewarned that any activity short of eating was forbidden, at least for the next few weeks. Now it looked as though he regretted setting the guidelines.

Now, weeks after the accident, she'd settled down, making herself at home as Logan instructed. He'd spent those weeks pampering her, making sure she recovered as thoroughly and comfortably as possible. His attention made her feel like royalty. When helping her dress, he respectfully looked away as he did when helping her towel off after a shower. His downfall, she learned, involved rubbing lotion on her back or brushing her hair. Halfway through she'd feel a soft, lingering kiss on the back of her neck or her shoulder.

He became adamant when she insisted on cooking or cleaning, instead demanding she rest and calling periodically through the day to ensure she *was* resting.

After so long, however, Sydney took matters to heart. It was unfair for Logan to house and feed her for nothing in return. Jason served as her taxi to and from work for those weeks, something else that grated on her nerves. No one allowed her to pay them back for *anything*. She'd remedy that soon, she vowed. For Jason, a check and a bouquet of carnations – his favorite. For Logan, the least she could do was cook and clean. He'd said she needed to exercise the hip more so why not be useful while exercising?

She started with the living room which remained remarkably clean. He kept his house spotless for a bachelor but then nothing was ordinary about Logan Calhoun. Regardless of his warnings, she was determined to earn her keep so she ran a dust cloth over things, polished glassware and ran the vacuum.

When she opened the door to his home office, the one room she hadn't seen yet, she took a moment to admire his work environment.

The room was painted cream with carpet the same color. The few pieces of furniture were heavy oak from his desk to the bookshelves lining two walls, four of the six packed full of classics and newer books. The shelves nearest the desk held medical and reference volumes. The remainder held other reference material and overflow from his living room shelves. Sydney estimated he owned hundreds of literature, poetry and history books, as well as a few fiction novels. While dusting the shelves, she noted that Shakespeare, Mark Twain and John Steinbeck were the most well worn and dog-eared. The longer she stayed, the more she learned about Logan. She discovered his penchant for history ranged from biblical to current day events, that his collection rivaled the Smithsonian and that he enjoyed the same poets as she.

Turning to the walls, a large print of Lady Godiva hung opposite his desk. The artist painted her from the side, her nude body tastefully covered by thick waves of dark hair. On a narrow wall next to the door, Logan hung his certificates and awards from University of Georgia Medical School and Georgia Baptist Medical Center, later Atlanta Medical Center. A proud smile curved her lips as she touched his name, "Logan Thomas Calhoun."

Along the wall behind his desk hung family photos. Each in matching dark wooden frames, all hung in a line across the wall. The first was a family photo. Hannah Calhoun hugged Logan close while Richard sat young Ethan on his shoulders. Sydney couldn't help notice they looked very happy together. At no more than six years old, Logan delighted in Hannah's affections, the boy in torn jeans and blue t-shirt hugged his mother proudly, the lifted chin and wicked grin pulled at

Sydney as it had, no doubt, Hannah. The same unruly lock of hair fell sinfully across his forehead, begging any available female to smooth it into place for a smile and sweet word of thanks. Even then Logan was a heartbreaker.

She dusted and polished the picture then moved to the next. Another of Logan and Hannah. He was older in this one and Sydney guessed it was one of the last photos he had of his mother. She recognized the shirt he wore from elementary school. The close-up revealed Logan favored his mother with a softer, more defined appearance whereas Ethan sported Richard's rugged, sharper features.

Hannah, in a simple but pretty peach dress, stood with Logan, who wrapped his mother in a bear hug. Young Logan glowed with adoration so strong, even a stranger could see it.

Sydney's heart ached for him. He missed his mother so much. The weeks they spent together he'd opened a chapter of his life he'd never shared before. The way his father treated his mother, the way she died, and the void in his heart that would never heal. Sydney learned Hannah was the reason Logan decided on a career in medicine. He wouldn't let another boy's mother suffer as his had, at the hands of a fraud.

Hannah's damaged spleen eventually failed due to Richard's numerous beatings. She'd fallen quite ill one day, prompting Logan to beg her to see a doctor. Richard, instead, insisted she see his "friend" who diagnosed the problem as an infection and prescribed rest and antibiotics. For several days, Logan religiously tended his mother before and after school until one day he walked in and found her lying on the floor. He'd kept calling her and through his tears pleaded for her to wake up. It was too late, Logan knew, but he called an ambulance anyway. He never forgave their father, he told Sydney one night. He likely never would.

Sydney remembered Mrs. Calhoun was nice and generous with compliments. The times she walked home with Ethan and Logan, Hannah invited Sydney in for ice cream. She'd shared dinner a few times with them, at Ethan's and Logan's behest. Hannah called her parents, assuring she would drive Sydney home herself afterward, "but the boys really want her to stay and she is such a delight to have around."

Wiping her own tears, Sydney recalled how Logan changed when Hannah passed away, becoming more reserved, selective with his outings to the point of becoming reclusive. Since their father spent most of his time either in jail or drunk, Logan took over parental responsibilities with Ethan. After hearing Logan's story, Sydney realized he sacrificed a lot for his brother and she hoped Ethan appreciated it.

Another picture showed Logan at his graduation from the University of Georgia Medical School. Ethan stood next to him, his arm slung around Logan's neck, a smug grin adorning his features. Ethan seemed proud of his brother. Sydney took pleasure in polishing each photo as she explored a different aspect of Logan's life. The pictures people hung on walls told a lot about them. Their past, the moments they shared with others. The family they displayed with honor.

She polished four more then the next photo, the last one, caught her by surprise. It was small in comparison, a five by seven – and it was of her. Sydney didn't touch her senior picture staring back at her. She looked at it with wonder and disbelief. Why did Logan hang her picture among the family photos? Sure, she and the Calhoun boys shared a past together but did it warrant this type of tribute, especially after she ran away – after she broke his heart?

She polished it anyway, still marveling at the concept. She gathered papers and straightened research and medical books, making certain everything stayed in proper order but with more room for him to work. The wastebasket, however, was Logan's Achilles' Heel. He'd managed to mound it over the top so nothing tumbled out. "This is as close to Mount Everest as I ever hope to get," she mumbled not as a complaint but as fact. It required talent to heap papers so perfectly.

Upending the basket into a large trash bag, she chuckled when several wadded pages bounced to the floor. Obviously she lacked his paper balancing talent. Sighing, she reached down to fetch them. About to release the fistful into the garbage sack, she stopped when a few words caught her eye. Not one to normally be nosy, she nearly tossed it away but something urged her to open the wad. "Thou and You…" it read.

Sydney's breath caught as she studied Logan's handwriting:

"She substituted, by a chance,

For empty "you" -- the gentle "thou";

And all my happy dreams, at once,

In loving heart again resound.

In bliss and silence do I stay,

Unable to maintain my role:

"Oh, how sweet you are!" I say --

"How I love thee!" says my soul."

She couldn't believe her eyes, "This is Alexander Pushkin." Excitement bolted up her spine knowing Logan enjoyed Pushkin too. But, upon closer examination of the handwriting, a realization slowly dawned on her. Over the past several weeks, she'd received many poems written in this flair. The formation of the letters, the masculine script style, reminiscent of calligraphy mixed with haste. She *knew* this writing.

Broken from her daze, Sydney pawed through the other papers like a dog digging for a bone. Sinking to her knees, she unfolded another and was glad she wasn't standing, "Petrarch," she said, her voice falling to a whisper. The poem "Bound To Love" lay in her now trembling hands – in Logan's writing. He'd made an error and marked it out and crumpled it in the trash. Sydney recalled every poem she received was perfectly written on the same thick, fibrous paper. She gutted the trash can again. Another poem graced her vision:

"I remember the wonderful moment;

Before me you appeared,

Like a passing vision,

Like a spirit of pure beauty..."

"Oh, Logan..." she wept, smiling through her tears. "It's you. *You're* Pushkin. You're my admirer." Sydney held the page to her heart, overwhelmed at his efforts, his persistence and his feelings for her. Even after she ran away from him, pleading with him to leave her alone, he still felt this deeply for her. Sydney couldn't control her tears now. She sat in the middle of the outrageously cluttered floor, spilling tears of joy.

23

The second Logan opened the front door, he noticed something different. Everything sparkled. The living room had been vacuumed, dusted and all the glass polished to gleaming. Stepping inside, it took one sniff to tell him Sydney hadn't just cleaned the house. He recognized this smell as one of his favorites. The rich aroma of chicken parmesan baking in the oven. The flavor of homemade spaghetti sauce wafted in the air, its zest tempered softly with mozzarella and parmesan. Memories of his mother's cooking invaded his brain. She'd always prepared the special meal for Logan as a surprise. Now with his mouth watering and his stomach yearning for the memorable feast, he wondered Sydney remembered that from their conversations. Then he wondered if she'd prepared the green salad along with it.

He heard the faint sound of humming. A happy little tune, except the song's name escaped him. Sydney's cheerfulness prompted a smile from him. He'd hoped she was content these past weeks. He really hoped she'd move in. The longer he waited to broach the subject the more he dreaded a possible rejection. Another painful rejection.

He hung his coat in the entry and followed the heavenly aroma to the kitchen. Logan saw Sydney, back turned to him, slicing romaine and butter lettuce. The corners of his mouth lifted in response. She remembered the salad. He leaned against the door frame, taking in the sight of her. Her attire was a fine appetizer to his visual hunger. A grape cotton tank top, the neckline plunging to expose the valley between her breasts, a fact he noted as she turned just enough to sip from her wine glass. The slender straps highlighted her kissable shoulders and delicate collarbones, two of her many features that caused him plenty of sleepless nights.

The pair of amethyst silk shorts accentuating her firm, round bottom temporarily hypnotized him. He could easily get accustomed to squeezing that very bottom currently sashaying back and forth in front of him. The apparel threw him. Sydney never dressed this temptingly in front of him. Since she stayed with him, her comfy attire consisted of jeans or shorts – shorts that hung to mid-thigh. Not these petite, hug-the-cheeks-and-drive-Logan-crazy-minis.

He watched while she lifted the glass of white wine again and sipped. God, he could stare at her forever. She shook her head once, tossing her hair to her back. Her bottom shimmered in the silk with the movement, begging him for attention. Logan's palms suddenly developed an itch. *This is not nice, Sydney. This is flat-out cruel. I should put you over my knee...* He groaned at the thought, knowing he was dying by degrees. That's when she turned, startled. What she did next startled *him*. She crossed her arms under her ample breasts, tilted her chin and beamed the most wicked grin he'd ever seen, "Welcome home, sweetheart," the timbre of her voice sank as deep and soft as the cleavage he craved to dive into. To polish him off, she finished, "I hope you're hungry."

Sydney made sure she prepared Logan's favorite meal that night. When he sighed and patted his stomach contentedly, she knew it pleased him. To reinforce the fact, he kept complimenting her cooking talents, something no other man ever did. She loved to cook and thought she was rather good at particular meals but to hear Logan rave about her abilities warmed her heart more than she expected. "I'm glad you enjoyed it," she said.

"It reminded me of my mother's cooking if that gives you any idea."

It did indeed. Logan cherished everything about his mother, including her cooking. She remembered watching him clean his plate and ask for seconds – sometimes thirds.

She rose from her seat and kissed him, "That is, quite possibly, the highest compliment anyone's given me. Thank you."

Logan caressed her cheek, "I noticed you cleaned the house too. You need to take it easy, sweetheart."

Her breath caught as his palm cradled her cheek. Her desire for Logan Calhoun only mounted since she'd stayed with him. Seeing him every day, waking up with his gentle kiss... "I've really enjoyed staying with you."

"Not half as much as I've enjoyed your company," he replied softly. He placed his napkin in his plate as though debating something.

A gentle smile curved her lips and she cupped his face in her palms, bringing his vision to hers, "I could live with you forever as special as I feel with you." She heard him exhale long and low.

Logan turned her palm up and kissed it, "That's the best news I've ever heard."

His off-handed response spurred her to nudge closer, her fingertips tracing his jaw, "I got some pretty outstanding news today too." They dropped to his collar, unbuttoned the top button. She saw his throat work at her bold move. She wanted to kiss that adorable knot that bobbed when he swallowed and put that at the top of her list.

The second button opened, the third and forth, exposing a wide expanse of chest, sprinkled generously with dark wisps of hair.

"What news?" he asked, his voice rough from her physical contact. Sydney secretly smiled inside, savoring his reaction. The longer her touch lingered, the more tremulous his breaths became.

Sydney slipped her hands inside his shirt, noting his warm skin growing moist with perspiration, "You'll find out."

Logan's breathing deepened, his eyelids descended leisurely as she eased her touch across his shoulders and downward through the dark carpet. He swallowed audibly, "Syd..."

"Yes, Logan?" her voice softened again.

His eyes opened in the same slow manner they'd closed, unveiling his indisputable passion for her. They lowered to her breasts that were level with them. She noticed he clearly focused on the nipples poking against the tank top. He spoke directly to them, "Don't start something you're unsure about. I don't want you to regret anything."

Sydney sank between his legs, hands settling on his knees and smiled, "This is one decision I'm positive I won't regret."

He started to respond when her hands eased up his thighs, choking off any rebuttal. The naughty grin she displayed while moving closer to his hips rendered him basically speechless. She saw his stomach clench when she touched his waist. Logan's fiery stare warned she should tread carefully now. Slowly, she inclined, placing a kiss at his navel.

Logan groaned long and loud. His fingers buried deep in her hair, urging her up to face him, "You're sure?"

Sydney tilted to press a kiss to his lips. She savored his sweet taste, yearning for more but not pushing just yet. Logan's hands trembled slightly as they cupped the back of her head. He wanted to believe her but he forced her to say the words. His reserved participation told the story. He'd only let himself go so far – until she gave permission. Until she agreed.

She barely parted the kiss and stared into passion so fierce, he both dared her to say no and prayed she didn't. Sydney nodded then quietly recited, "I loved you: and, it may be, from my soul; The former love has never gone away…"

Initially, she could tell the prose confused Logan. Then word by word the fog parted. "Pushkin?" he asked.

"Indeed," she nodded, smiled.

Wary, he studied her expression. The bigger her smile grew, the more he evidently realized she recognized her admirer's identity, "You figured out it was me?"

She nodded. Logan searched her green eyes, "How long have you known?"

"That was *my* great news.   I found out today when I was cleaning."   She kissed him briefly, "You should empty your trash more often."

The beginnings of a grin eased his worried appearance as she quietly murmured, "Vorrei trascorrere tutta la mia vita con te."

These were *her* feelings in Italian she watched him mentally translate the meaning.   Suddenly, his eyes sparkled as he swept her into his arms, "I would like to spend all my life with you too."

24

Sydney loved dressing comfortably for work. Since George Kelso heard about her accident, he'd given her permission to dress in sweaters, jeans and sneakers. She could get accustomed to this, she thought with a smile. She'd realized in the past weeks that George wasn't as lecherous as she'd first thought. As Jason predicted, once he understood she was attached, he'd left strictly alone except for business and advice. He dropped by occasionally to check up on her and give her tips on what medication worked best on pain. He'd learned the hard way, he said, since a college injury to his left hip caused him many sleepless nights. "Football?" she'd asked.

"No," he'd then hesitated. "Beer. I got drunk and fell over the balcony, landed on my left side and life was never the same so take care of yourself."

She'd tried but Logan took it further, as if she was made of porcelain. Even that morning, he'd taken breakfast duty and ordered her to sit down. Now with a joyful, reflective sigh, she resumed her work. After spending thirty minutes perusing the new load of manuscripts, Sydney decided on one. The new author really showed potential, according to the initial evaluation. Upon reading the first chapter, she wholeheartedly agreed.

By the second chapter, she was completely enthralled. Rose brought her a cup of coffee and she'd absently thanked her, and Jason brought papers and contracts in without her barely noticing. She'd even heard the faint wail of sirens outside, she thought, but nothing broke her concentration from the book.

Something now, however, demanded her attention. Jason and Rose both stood directly in front of her desk looking positively distraught. Rose looked scared and Jason hesitant. Sydney's eyes rounded, "What is it?" Their emotions seemed to transfer to her, making her stomach tense.

Jason, as always, approached subjects cautiously. "Honey, you didn't hear the sirens?"

Rose, on the other hand, barreled in like a bull, "Have you listened to the radio this morning?"

All Sydney could do was shake her head. "What *is* it?" She now demanded pushing to her feet. She didn't like the anxiousness flooding her system. The sheer dread. Whatever it was, Jason faltered too long. His lips parted to answer but Rose stepped to the cabinet behind Sydney's desk and switched on the radio. Another wave of muffled sirens filtered in through the window where Rose pointed, "More police cars."

Sydney looked out the window. The police cruisers sped past the Fantasy building, sirens and lights going full bore. They zipped down Peachtree and out of her sight. The radio revealed the mystery, "At this hour the hostage situation continues at Atlanta Medical Center.

According to witnesses, a gunman entered the emergency entrance around seven-thirty this morning. No one has exited the building except one doctor with a gunshot wound to the shoulder. He was transported to Grady Memorial where he's listed in stable condition. Police have cordoned off the three block perimeter around the hospital and are advising people to stay clear of the area. We will have more details as they become available."

"Logan," she cried. He'd left early for the morning shift in the ER. A five o'clock phone call woke them both. A doctor had fallen ill and couldn't work his shift. The caller asked Logan to take the remainder of the shift despite the fact it extended Logan's by a few hours. Always wanting to help where possible, Logan had agreed. Awake by that time, Sydney rolled out of bed with him and they'd shared a quick breakfast. Then, thinking Logan was about to leave, she jumped in the shower to clean up. To her surprise, he'd lingered outside the shower then swung the door open to give her an unusual but very stimulating good-bye. They'd parted with plans for that night. Plans Sydney ran point by point through her tormented brain. She wouldn't leave Logan all alone. She had to be there for him. The radio said Grady Memorial which wasn't far from Atlanta Medical. From Fantasy, it was a twenty minute trip if traffic and weather permitted.

Turning to leave, she ran straight into Jason's arms, "Honey, Logan wasn't shot. I finally got the information from a friend at Grady."

Relief briefly washed over her features only to be replaced by the same powerful fear, "He's still in danger. I have to go to him."

She struggled to free herself but his hold tightened, "You can't,

Sydney. The police won't allow it. I know you want to be with Logan but staying here is the best option. Believe me, honey."

"Please drive me to the hospital." She grasped his shirt in her fists, tears rolling down her cheeks, "Please, take me."

Jason glanced at Rose for help. Rose just shrugged. Frustrated with his delay, Sydney tore free and ran, grabbing her purse on the way out, "I'll get a cab."

"Sydney!" he called, his voice unexpectedly imposing. His authoritative tone halted her, like a father's reprimand stopped a child. He marched toward her, taking her arm, "I'll drive you but you cannot pass the police barrier. You will be arrested and you can't help Logan if you're in jail."

25

Within the hour, the sky darkened with storm clouds. Distant flashes of lightning promised a wicked storm would roll into the city soon. The clouds boiled in places, gradually transforming the spring thunderstorm dove gray to a menacing raven. A shiver raked Sydney's spine. First the crisis at the hospital, now threatening storms.

The nine mile trip felt excruciatingly long as numerous nightmare scenarios tormented her. One after the other, each scene became bloodier and deadlier than the last. The only thing ceasing the frightening images was Jason's touch on her arm. As they drove down McGill, she noted how business continued as usual, people smiling and talking as though a crisis hadn't gripped a major institution in the city. Video stores, supermarkets, gas stations, all busy, the patrons seemingly unaware.

Sydney wasn't. Her heart twisted painfully in her chest. Logan *had* to be okay. Jason turned onto Parkway and the atmosphere changed. People began lining the sidewalks, some walking toward Atlanta Medical Center.

More people gathered the closer they came to the police

perimeter, gawking and pointing at the hospital. The bizarre situation blanked Sydney's mind except for Logan. As the barrier approached, she grew more restless. She needed to be near him. With him.

The uniformed officer pointed to the curb. Obeying, Jason veered over and stopped. They were three blocks from the hospital, so close Sydney saw the building's white block lettering clearly across the top, so close she saw the building framed by the looming storm, the clouds boiling behind it. So close she swore she felt Logan's heart racing.

The officer approached, signaling him to roll the window down, "The street's closed. You'll have to circle back."

"Yes, Officer," Jason acknowledged and shifted into Reverse. Suddenly the passenger door flew open to his horror, making him stomp the brake, "Sydney!"

She pushed through the initial wave of onlookers as the cop zeroed in on her, "Ma'am, get back in the car." To his surprise, she continued fighting her way through the crowd now opening a path for her. She dashed into the nearest alley for a shortcut, her feet pounding through puddles and crunching over shattered beer bottles. The thick, oppressive air weighed her lungs down as she ran. She strained for breath against the humidity just as her muscles strained for more speed. Her right hip ached slightly, warning her to slow down but she couldn't. Logan needed her. After two blocks, she heard a breathless plea behind her, "Sydney, wait for me!"

Again, Jason's tone demanded compliance and her pace slowed, "Don't try to stop me."

He took her arm, spinning her to him, "Listen to me. I know

you love Logan but be rational. If you interfere, you might jeopardize the police's work. Doing that jeopardizes Logan." Now he tenderly swept her tears away, "Stay out of it, honey."

She lifted her gaze as more tears fell. At the sight, Jason's stern demeanor melted and he drew her into his arms, "Let the police will work it out."

Sydney held hard to him. She wanted to believe him. Common sense told her the police dealt with these situations all the time. Then an idea occurred to her, pulling her from Jason's embrace, "Maybe Ethan's here. He can help." She took off again and left Jason shaking his head while struggling to catch his breath. When she finally reached the command center set up across from the ER, she looked at every uniformed cop, searching for Ethan.

Unfortunately, Ethan found her first, "Well, if it isn't our lawbreaker." The patronizing tone caught several officers' interest. They turned in his direction, seeing him swagger toward Sydney, "I heard you jumped the perimeter and disobeyed a direct order to stop. 'Zat true?"

Sydney instantly realized Ethan would provide nothing but a hard time, especially when an arrogant smile crept into his features. She hoped with his brother in peril he'd act like an adult. It seemed, however, the mere sight of her provoked his immature nature to blossom full force. Now he directed her attention to his badge, arrogantly stating, "You're playing by *my* rules now. I tell you to put your hands behind your back and you say, 'Yes, Lieutenant Calhoun'. *And you do it.*"

His pompous attitude incensed her but she swallowed the feeling and brought forth her most determined tone, "I'm going in there whether you approve or not. Logan needs help." She swiveled on her right heel and immediately cringed when a twinge raked through her hip and leg. The sharp pain radiated from her waist to her ankle, scattering all conscious thought. She cradled it then gasped when a large, strong grip seized the wrist and twisted her toward the trunk of a cruiser. Her hips struck the back fender, pain wrenching a cry from her lips.

Ethan had a point to make and now possessed the authority to enforce it. His hips solidly nailed hers against the white cruiser, forcibly pinning her. Sydney whimpered from the jarring motion, "Damn it, back off. That hurts."

Overlooking the complaint, he leaned closer to her ear while strengthening his hold, "You are *not* going in there. If you persist, I'll throw cuffs on you and toss your ass in jail, this time for real."

The pain subsided enough to resurface her temper, "He needs me."

"Well, I warned you." Ethan's hand flattened on her back and bent her over the trunk. Sydney turned before her chin struck the trunk, her vision met Jason's hopeless expression. He obviously hadn't a clue what to do as Ethan announced, "It gives me such great pleasure to do this, Ms. Eatonton. You are now under arrest." He snapped a handcuff on her left wrist and spoke through a smile, "You have the right to remain silent…"

She writhed against him, "Let me go, Ethan. Don't you understand–"

"I understand plenty. I understand you've disobeyed two officers. I understand you want inside the hospital. I also understand you're going to jail and if your assistant doesn't go with Officer Dunning, he'll share the cell with you." Ethan nabbed her forearm, twisted and brought it behind her. Sydney cried at the pain radiating from the still healing wound and Ethan's duty belt grinding against her hip. Feeling the cold metal click into place, she impaled him with words, "The guy's already shot one doctor. What happens if he shoots Logan? Your pride is more important than your brother?" She gasped when his fist doubled in her shirt and he physically hauled her upright, turned her and drilled her with cold narrowed eyes. His right eye twitched and his face flushed. She felt herself drawing back from Ethan who gnashed his teeth, "Dunning, take Ms. Eatonton downtown and introduce her to our new fingerprinting system. Make sure to get a nice, pretty picture of her too."

A massive uniform officer built like a sturdy brick wall took her arm but she shrugged free of his hold. She wasn't nearly finished with Ethan. Dunning bounced an uncertain glance between the two, as if he'd interrupted a lover's quarrel. When she spoke, he smartly stepped back. Staring into Ethan's hardened features, she prodded him again, "I thought you had a heart somewhere in that thick-headed, egotistical body."

Jason stepped between them, speaking timidly, "Excuse me, Lieutenant Calhoun, but I'm sure Sydney will listen to reason if you will spare her the arrest." He frowned at her, "Won't you?"

Ethan's condescending laugh died in the sultry air. He looked past Jason to her, "Oh sure. She'll listen to me. I tell her to stay put and *she'll run inside that hospital*." He focused on Dunning once more, "Take her before I do something that gets my ass suspended."

This time, Dunning took Sydney's arm firmly while Ethan addressed Jason, "She'll need someone to post bail. Call Samantha because Sydney won't."

Dunning led her to a nearby cruiser with her still straining against the handcuffs. She willed the chain to break so she could strangle Ethan, "At least I'd try to save Logan," she shot over her shoulder. "Instead of being a pompous ass wielding a badge and throwing my official weight around. All while doing *nothing*. That's your brother in there, for God's sake."

Heavy footfalls pounded the asphalt behind her. Several voices called Ethan down but he heeded none. She heard more people running at the same time a sharp pain registered near her shoulder. Large, blunt fingertips burrowed into the soft flesh of her upper arm, halting her and Dunning. Numerous officers forcibly restrained Ethan, pulling her back and away from her. He pierced her with his eyes and his words, the latter crushing between his teeth, "I know that. I also know you share his bed when you should be sharing mine."

A nearby officer finally piped up, "You two bitch at each other like you're married."

Both turned, barking in unison, "Shut up." They stared, again daring the other to further the nasty sparring match. After a moment, Sydney's eyes widened as yet another idea formed.

Somehow reading her mind, Ethan shook his head while retreating from her. He registered unadulterated fear like she'd threatened to light him on fire, "No, Sydney. There's no way in hell and you can't make me..."

26

Logan stayed perched on a cabinet in the ER. He adjusted his hips again, praying the feeling returned to his rear soon. His tailbone thoroughly ached from sitting. For the past six hours, he and eleven others crowded the small room, some sitting on the floor, others on the cabinet and table. Three doctors, eight nurses and one patient with a puncture wound to his foot. The air felt warm and sticky, especially since the ER doors were closed and locked. He thought he heard distant thunder earlier. Now the storm approached viciously, thunder rattled instruments and glass containers, the lights blinked occasionally, adding to the gunman's irritation.

All in all, the staff held up well, especially the women, except one young nurse worried him. She cried easily, something the gunman detested. Logan made sure to keep eye contact with her, visually reassuring her, trying to calm her.

Being the eldest staff member present, Logan tried to stay composed, even when the gunman shot Dr. Williams. He urged everyone to stay quiet and managed to convince the man to release the doctor but that was early in the game. Now the gunman, Shaun, showed signs of mental and emotional wear along with the staff.

He'd rushed in shortly after seven that morning, ordering some people out, ordering others to stay then ushered them into a small ER cubicle.   Waving the gun wildly, the twenty-something year-old dedicated a good half hour ranting about an operation gone awry. His sister died from a failed heart valve replacement and he wanted a life for a life. Dr. Elliot, the doctor who'd fallen ill, was the surgeon's life he wanted.

For the most part Shaun stayed at the door of the ER, flailing the gun erratically at anyone who spoke or looked like they might.   Dr. Williams had simply moved too fast for his liking. After releasing him to the police, Shaun made one final warning. Anyone that moved without his or her hands fully in view would be killed, not injured. The remaining staff believed him, especially Logan. The boy's eyes displayed a glazed wildness, like a drug user coming off a bad high. The brooding turbulence that erupted into brutal violence in a mere split second told Logan revenge would be exacted on anyone crossing him.

Logan wiped his hand down his face, ridding himself of the fine sheen of sweat. It fast approached roasting temperature in the small room and everyone wore light sweaters or warmer clothing anyway. A picture of Sydney's smile eased his discomfort. He'd left that morning with her still in the shower. He stepped into the bathroom and waited for the steam to dissipate. Through the glass door he saw poetry in motion as she rinsed her hair, the shampoo skimming down the graceful slope of her back. He remembered washing her hair for her after her release, then brushing it slowly, reverently until she grew tired and sleepy.

Logan let a smile emerge. They'd planned on a romantic evening when he got home. Impromptu plans made as hot steam enveloped them, shrouding them in wet heat. Before sliding his black oxford shirt on, he opened the shower door and kissed her, vowing, "Tonight you're mine."

"I'm yours every night," she'd replied, her lips brushing his.

Sitting on the cabinet, he shifted his hips as his body reacted to the memory. If he made it home alive, Sydney would never sleep again. He'd make sure of it. He wanted Shaun to end this stand-off so everyone could return to their families and the ER could resume business. People were possibly dying while ambulances re-routed to other hospitals like Grady Memorial and Crawford Long.

A voice in the hallway – Shaun's – caught his attention. The young man's agitated tone sharpened, "Stop. I said stop or I'll shoot! What the hell's wrong with you? Didn't you see the cops outside?"

"My wife and I were in an accident and she hurt her leg. She needs help."

A bell of recognition rang in Logan's mind like an alarm. He knew the man and also recognized the female moans and whimpers. Logan slowly angled to glance out the door. Terror filled his heart and his brain upon seeing Ethan and Sydney. Sucking in a shaky breath, he flattened his back against the wall, cradling his head in his hands. What did these two think they were doing?

Incapable of showing anything short of maliciousness, Shaun mocked Ethan's tone, "She needs help." Logan heard Shaun approach them, his voice growling, "Since I'm the doc on duty, I'll help her. I'll put her out of her misery right now."

A shot rang out and Logan panicked. Suddenly weakened and strangely energized by a flood of adrenaline, he leapt off the cabinet. If Shaun hurt Sydney, he wouldn't know the meaning of pain until Logan got hold of him. His large form filled the doorway, startling Shaun who raised the weapon chest level with Logan, "Chill, asshole. Everything's under control."

Logan's alarmed expression settled on Sydney lying in Ethan's arms. The air escaped his lungs in a rush. She was okay. His knees wobbled, his heart nearly stopped. Thank God she wasn't hurt but if they survived this, he swore to put her over his knee and give her the spanking her daddy never did. She'd learn not to put herself in harm's way again.

The phone began ringing for the hundredth time. The cops heard the shot. Shaun wouldn't pick up, he hadn't for the last two hours and at the moment he seemed too enchanted with the fear coursing behind Sydney's eyes.

Logan surveyed the scene. Ethan, dressed in a coral sweater and tan Dockers, held Sydney in his arms, and both wore wedding rings. The image was as surreal as seeing a gun waved in his face – and equally as disturbing. Sydney's saucered eyes wavered between terror and pain, a pain Logan sensed was real, however negligible.

His vision locked on Sydney who whimpered again, quietly complaining about her leg. Logan's hands lifted as Shaun ordered and he tried to make eye contact with Ethan. Ethan just nodded toward Sydney. Logan nearly collapsed. This was her idea – and the cops sent her in anyway? Second on his list was lodging a formal complaint against the police for needlessly endangering a citizen.

Logan swallowed dryly and tried to urge the couple to leave, "Grady Memorial is about a mile and a half southwest of here. Take your wife there. Please."

The ringing phone became insistent. Shaun's wire-thin patience waned behind clenched teeth. He remained motionless except shifting the gun from the couple to Logan, trying to decide what to do.

Sydney cried into Ethan's shoulder nearly causing Logan to faint. Shaun's fuse shortened dramatically when a woman cried. He'd seen firsthand the barrel pressed against soft female flesh and couldn't bear to witness Sydney in that position.

As he feared Shaun focused on her with the gun. His dull vision narrowed, his patience with her was nil, "I got what'll cure ya, bitch. If ya don't want to eat a bullet then shut up!"

Sniffing back the tears, she called for Logan, "Please help me."

The insistence wore Shaun to the last thread, Logan knew. She may have dried the tears but Shaun wanted complete silence. Between the storm, phone and her, their gunman danced on the edge of uncontainable rage. Logan tried to silently warn her to shut up when Ethan groused, "She's getting heavy. At least let me put her down, you know, or we could just leave." He shrugged to wipe a trail of sweat from his jaw, mumbling, "God, woman, lose a few after this."

Logan shot daggers at Ethan for opening his mouth. Shaun skimmed the gun's barrel down her cheek, caressing, "You ain't goin' nowhere." His stare penetrated Ethan, "Put her on that table." Then lowered his sight to Sydney, "Then we'll get to know each other personally. We'll even let your old man watch."

The incessant ringing phone tightened Shaun's jaw, fed his temper. He bolted to the cabinet, lifted the receiver, "Until you give me Elliot, don't bother calling." He glanced at Sydney, "Besides, I've got plenty of entertainment here while you round him up," then slammed the phone down. A loud crack of thunder rolled through the hospital, causing the lights to blink precariously. The room dimmed slightly as storm clouds blackened the sky outside.

Logan cleared his throat, hands still raised. Shaun wheeled, his teeth bared, "What is it, doc? I'm busy."

"May I have a look at her leg? She obviously needs medical attention."

"Make it fast. We got plans, me and her."

He slowly approached them with hands lifted. The closer Logan got, the angrier he grew. Then he felt the gun's barrel against his back. He pointed to the same gurney, instructing Ethan, "Put her here. Gently." The last word emerged as his own warning. Ethan looked none too pleased to be carrying her.

Ethan placed Sydney on the gurney and was promptly shoved away by Shaun, "Let him work. I don't like it when people hover."

Logan reached for a pair of gloves and snapped them on. The set in his jaw and pursed lips screamed his displeasure at her presence. The deadly fury in his expression should have sent her running, an action he sensed coursing through her. Before she moved, his hand grasped her jaw firmly while retrieving his pen light, "Now, Mrs...."

"Thomas," she uttered, the pulse pounding frantically against her neck. Logan nearly smiled at the throbbing heartbeat and the name she'd used. His middle name. "Mrs. Thomas. Can you tell me what happened?" He kept his voice just loud enough for Shaun to hear. He listened to the story she told and leaned closer to her while flashing the light in her ear, whispering, "You're both insane. You need to get out."

Her mouth opened but he stopped her, "Just be quiet. I'm going to check you over and send you out, if it's not too late." He leaned against her ear, "If he'll let you go, you'd better damn well go. Understand?"

Sydney let him roll her head to face him, his grasp still firm on her jaw. It tightened slightly, "*Do you understand?*"

Her vision blazed with stern determination and the muscles clenched beneath his hold. She wouldn't leave him, her expression said, and nothing he did short of physically booting her out would work.

Logan's brow sank, hardening his features.

Sydney's eyes widened, their aim passing over his shoulder. Shaun's voice broke the tension only to bump it to a new level, "Got a secret, doc? Share it with the class."

Cold metal pushed under the back of Logan's skull. He straightened slowly but surely with no sudden movement. Shaun nudged the barrel forward, prompting for an answer. Logan closed his eyes, took a deep breath and willed his heart to stop pounding. Getting shot, especially in front of Sydney, wasn't in the plan. "I always ask the patient certain questions to rule out a concussion."

Shaun wasn't convinced, "What isn't she understanding?"

Sydney took Logan's lead, this time wincing with discomfort from his hold, "I'll be still from now on. Sorry."

The gunman lowered the muzzle, scolding, "Your bedside manner sucks, doc. You always intimidate your patients? Let her go."

Logan's lips trembled with ire. He wanted this monster away from Sydney and wanted to shake sense into her and convince her to leave. He released her as Shaun wheeled unexpectedly, "Sit down, asshole, unless you want your wife to be a widow."

Ethan's voice sounded too close when he uttered his apology. Both Sydney and Logan realized he'd tried to ambush Shaun. Another wave of weakness surged through Logan. His brother would cock it up and get them all killed, "Sit down, sir. We've got plenty of problems as it is," he instructed.

The rain fell hard now. Pounding the pavement outside in waves, pea-sized hailstones plinked the windows then replaced the rain entirely. The sound echoed through the ER like a giant truck dumping a load of pebbles on the hospital. The noise unnerved Shaun who backed toward the cabinet. The phone rang was ringing again and this time he picked up, "Where's Elliot? You've got thirty minutes to march his ass through those doors or people start dying."

Logan took advantage of the brief private moment. He tilted her head to look in the other ear, "I have an idea to get out of this mess..."

27

"Hurry it up, Doc," Shaun demanded, edging in closer to Logan and Sydney. He wiped his face with the tail of his salmon colored shirt then haphazardly tucked it into his well worn jeans. His shaking fingers combed through his mass of oily blond hair. After a decent haircut and shave, he'd have probably passed as a wiry teenager but right now he looked and acted like absolute evil.

Sydney's vision swept across his wild features, his tight mouth, flared nostrils and squinted bloodshot eyes. Eyes that appeared rust-brown earlier but now clouded into inky wells behind the red-rimmed lids.

Size-wise, Logan and Ethan stood taller and broader than he. In contrast, the pint-sized time bomb stood about her height, his slight build carried sparse muscle and looked rather anemic and malnourished, the latter no doubt a result of years of drug abuse. Muscle or not, the carelessly waving gun and his fast souring attitude made people listen and act – except Logan who still remained calm, "Exams take a while."

Sydney watched Shaun lean to Logan's ear, the menacing smile spreading as he whispered, "Speed it up. After I'm done with her, I might let you have a piece too. Would you like that, doc?"

Sydney sensed Logan's fury building. A slight tremor in his hand and the tensing at the corners of his eyes warned of an explosion of monumental proportions. She'd seen this look – or its next of kin – sixteen years ago. He'd hit a tree bare-fisted then. She dreaded to think what would happen now.

Making solid eye contact with Logan, she touched his hand. As though the gentle caress comforted him, he drew a breath, his focus returned and he squeezed her hand. The grasp tightened as Shaun pushed his week old beard against Logan's left ear, taunting, "I'll bet she's sweet." Then let a low, short laugh, "We'll have ourselves a party, wha'dya think, doc?"

Flames virtually erupted behind Logan's narrowed vision. Sydney gripped him hard, attempting to contain his anger and begging him to stay calm. Shaun deliberately provoked him, sensing Logan danced on a fine line of lashing out.

"She's been in an accident and requires medical treatment," Logan launched his words viciously at him. "Your purpose for being here isn't to assault women, it's something entirely different as I recall."

Logan glanced at Sydney. Uncertainty carved itself in her brow. Shaun wasn't taking the outburst well. He stared at Logan, his breaths short and shallow as if his brain formulated an answer but his body's reaction time fell behind. When his body caught up, however, it scared the hell out of them all.

A loud shot rang out, and Sydney clamped a shriek behind her lips and Logan leaned in close, shielding her. He cringed as her fingernails sank into his palm then covered her hand, squeezing to reassure her, "It's okay, babe. It's okay," he murmured lowly.

Ethan drew back on the bench, "Holy shit, man, be careful with that," his wobbly voice pleaded.

Shaun wheeled, aiming at him, "Shut up. I need something to take the edge off." The gun swung to Logan, "And you're gonna give me one."

"One what?" Logan still hovered over Sydney protectively, his frown meeting Shaun's pale, sweaty expression. He watched the man drag his forearm across his upper lip, then his free hand down his face. A bright flash immediately followed by a crashing sound startled them all. If Ethan didn't get them killed, Logan surmised, the storm would. Every time it thundered, Shaun's tremors worsened.

"Demerol." Shaun stated gruffly, "It'll settle the shakes and *none* of you want me to have those."

"No shit," Ethan mumbled.

Shaun remained stone still, the words squeezing through gnashed teeth, "One more word and you're dead."

A knowing look passed between Logan and Sydney. Instead of Demerol, Logan would draw up a fast-acting sedative and finally end the terrifying showdown once and for all. With Shaun asking for the medication, it would be much easier than Logan's original plan of overpowering him and injecting him with the sedative.

As if reading their thoughts, Shaun motioned to Logan, "Now I ain't takin' no injection shit. You'll pull a stupid and I know it. Get me two Demerol *pills*."

Sydney silently cursed but Logan nodded, evidently still seeing an opportunity, "May I draw up medication for Mrs. Thomas? Something to relieve her pain?"

The man's eyes darted between the three. Fatigue wore heavy in his features. Prominent beads of sweat dripped down his forehead and neck. Outlines of heavy perspiration ringed the underarms of his t-shirt and a broad stripe formed in the middle of his chest and back. A drug addict wielding a gun was bad enough but one coming off a high had to be worse. At this rate, Shaun would grow more volatile, she feared. She wasn't mistaken.

Shaun raised the barrel to her temple and cocked the hammer, "Sure, doc. Just don't do anything dumb. She wants to keep her brains *inside* her head," he glanced at her, "don't you?"

Sydney spoke softly, "Preferably, yes." Her heart raced and she struggled for a steady breath with the cold metal pressed at her temple. Without Logan present, retaining her control was challenging at best with a cocked .45 wedged against her skull.

Logan turned back to her, forcing a calm demeanor. He directed his response to her, "Don't worry. I'll be right back."

As he started toward the ER, Ethan meandered toward the two. Sydney pierced him with an incredulous glare, warning him not to press the situation. As a result, Shaun solidly drove the barrel into her flesh, the pressure forcing her head onto her right ear. Her whimper broke the silence and Shaun addressed Ethan, "You're deaf, aren't ya, smart-ass? I told you to *sit down*."

Ethan *had* to see Sydney's heartbeat fluttering beneath her sweater and the pulse hammering in her neck, didn't he? She felt close to hyperventilating and if Ethan didn't back down, she was convinced Shaun would shoot her simply for "marrying" an idiot.

Ethan looked at Shaun, "I have to pee. Can I go pee?"

"Ethan," Sydney whimpered, her plea punctuated with a painful cringe, "not now."

Ethan frowned at her, "You're telling me when I can and can't pee?"

Shaun put a hand securely across Sydney's throat as he swung the gun at Ethan, "No, *I'm* telling you when you can and can't pee. And you cannot go pee."

"Sit down," the voiceless plea eked past her constricted throat.

"Sit your ass down *now*." He transferred his aim back to Sydney who gasped at the chill of the barrel sinking into her temple.

The sharp, deafening sound of thunder split the silence. Shaun's grip on the trigger quivered as she trembled from fear. The storm sat on top of the hospital, pouring so hard sheets of rain raked the windows and ER doors. Glancing sideways, Sydney noticed the street darkened to night from the storm. The pelting hail grew in size and developed into a definitive, deep roar that resounded through the room, unnerving them all. Occasionally larger hailstones soared past the windows like missiles and landed with a noise akin to boulders falling from the sky.

Glass breaking nearby jangled everyone's nerves. The intermittent sound of upstairs windows shattering along with Ethan's bull-in-a-china-closet personality and Shaun's volatility about sealed her fate. She was convinced she wouldn't die from a gunshot wound. She would expire due to stress.

Ethan pointed downward, ensuring she saw him. He'd strapped his backup weapon to his ankle, she knew that but somehow the knowledge didn't comfort her. Ethan's propensity for bad timing and his temper always doomed him. And now she, Logan and several others were at his mercy. The borrowed tan Dockers fit loosely on him and if he walked carefully, no one saw the holstered weapon, "I gotta go or my pipe'll burst. You know I can't hold it, love."

She gritted her teeth at the subtle gibe but mostly because she felt Shaun's hand shaking again. Images of her family flashed in her mind, memories of holidays together, and of future occasions to be enjoyed. She didn't want to die. There were too many days she intended to share with Logan and her family. Dying wasn't an option but trying to convey the information visually to Ethan either apparently went ignored or he wasn't catching on. He was testing the gunman at her expense. If he wasn't naturally deficient of common sense, she'd swear he did it on purpose. Her only hope was Logan. She couldn't bring herself to making eye contact with Shaun but said, "He won't hush until he pees."

Shaun leaned closer, a bead of sweat dropped onto her cheek, "I have a surefire way of shutting him up, *love,* but I'm betting he doesn't want to watch me blow your head off." Without looking away, he waved Ethan to the cabinet, "Piss in the trash. You make one wrong move, I'll kill her and make you watch."

Some threat, Sydney thought ironically. The way Ethan treated her outside, he'd probably sell tickets to the event. But interestingly, the way he moved, watching her die didn't appeal to him either. With slow, distinct movements, he lowered the zipper on his trousers.

Her eyes closed in prayer. Prayer that Ethan kept his cool and didn't try reaching for the gun through his damn fly. She prayed that Logan emerged before Ethan's backup weapon.

Shaun's hand trembled more now, his finger contracting on the trigger. If he sensed anything amiss, her life was over.

A soft sound brought her eyes open. Logan clearing his voice. *Thank God.* "I've got your pain med, Mrs. Thomas."

Shaun pivoted while pressing the weapon soundly at her temple, "And mine?"

"Yours as well." He extended a cup with two rather large red capsules. Shaun stared fiercely at the cup, studying the medication, "I swear, doc, you screw me over and I'll kill you and your family."

"Two Demerol," he recited. "It's what you asked for." Logan's deep, steady voice reassured Sydney slightly. Whether or not he was actually in control, his voice said he was. He still had a plan. She watched as Logan calmly extended a glass of water, his dark eyes never straying from Shaun's.

"Gosh thanks, Doc," he grabbed the cup with the pills. The tremors were worse, Sydney noticed, watching his efforts to successfully tilt the cup to his mouth. Then he downed the remainder of water with some trailing down the sides of his mouth onto his shirt. A fierce glare shadowed his dark eyes, "Now hers."

Logan slowly reached into his white coat to withdraw a syringe. He saw her shivering, terrified of Shaun's unsteady grip on the weapon. He exchanged a composed glance with her, letting her know not to panic.

Logan spoke softly despite the visible rage boiling beneath the surface, "Excuse me, but since I'm back, maybe you could stop pointing the gun at her."

Sydney watched Ethan bend down for the backup weapon. While Logan diverted Shaun's attention, she observed Ethan retrieve the weapon then watched him slide the small snubnose into his pocket. A visual plea passed between the two and he nodded.

Shaun's lip curled, "Does it look like I'm gonna listen? You and your friends in there serve as collateral only. These two are my best insurance. Cops really hate for citizens to die. Since they didn't see the happy couple come in or they'd have stop..." His sentence halted abruptly as if his brain stumbled on an answer. A brief moment passed as the realization slowly dawned.

Logan eased his hand into his coat again but Shaun saw him, "Keep your friggin' hands where I can see them." His vision lowered to Sydney, "You two *are* cops."

"I'm not a cop," she whispered. "My husband and I were in an accident –"

"You look mighty good for being in a wreck." He pressed the gun deeper, "You'll tell me the truth one way or another." He nodded to Ethan. "Is he a cop?"

Sydney cried out from the pressure. Through pained eyes, she locked on Ethan, "He's my husband." A subtle wave of relief washed over Ethan, she noticed, but Shaun turned a deaf ear. Wrapping his hand around her throat, he pulled her to a sitting position, the gun now shoved under her chin, "You two don't act married. Take the ring off."

She twisted the borrowed diamond off her hand. Shaun glared at her, "Lift your hand."

"May I give her the pain medication?" Logan interrupted. His tone now revealed a hint of fear. The thread of alarm wound its way to her and blossomed full force. She needed a way to divert his attention away from the men so they could overpower him.

Shaun cut his eyes to the side, "No. We're not done here, are we, *love*? Show me your hand."

Sydney raised her left hand and she knew by his reaction, he recognized the truth. A sinister smile crept across his lips now, "Just like I figured. You're both cops and since I like you best, you get to play my game."

She didn't answer. She didn't look at Logan but focused only on Shaun. Her silence only exaggerated his grin, "Since your buddies won't take me seriously, maybe if they know their sweet girl is getting hers, they'll listen. 'Course they don't have to listen too close 'cause they'll hear your screams." Shaun's hand fisted in her hair while swinging the gun to the men, "You two, on the bench now." He uttered no command for Sydney. His grip instructed her as he shoved her to her knees, his strength wrenching a cry from her throat.

Both brothers struggled to make eye contact with Sydney but she refused to meet their worried vision. If she made eye contact with Logan, she'd fall completely apart and Shaun would shoot her on the spot.

Keeping his attention trained on the men, Shaun nodded to her, "Open my pants, bitch. See what you're gettin'. Do something stupid and I'll kill you slowly."

Sydney's shaking hands gradually reached to his jeans. The worn buttonholes were easy to maneuver, a little too easy for her taste. Her breaths trembled as glaringly as her hands. Working the Levis open, she lifted her vision to the gun. She wondered how far she could actually go with this charade since the gun stayed trained on the men. She couldn't endanger them by attacking Shaun but she wasn't about to allow the madman to rape her either.

She hesitated, he tightened his hold in her hair, making her cringe. He ordered, "Keep working."

Sydney slowed her progress and Shaun slapped her hand away, "I'll do it for you then." He took the button side of the fly and yanked. The fly popped open like mere Velcro held it together.

Sitting on her knees, Sydney stared at the bulging arousal in his briefs. This situation surpassed six degrees of hideous and soared past seven. His hand returned to her hair, "Stand up. I'll show you how I undress bitches like you."

Sydney screamed as he yanked her hair. The lights blinked with another round of thunder just as Shaun lunged forward – someone pushed him, she assumed. Then she saw Logan tackle Shaun flat. The room lights continued to flicker as the two struggled for the gun and Ethan scrambled to help his brother.

A deafening shot rang out then Sydney heard it. Heard *him*. Logan groaned deep and long, a mournful groan. Twisting to right herself, she struggled to stand only to be met with a gun barrel to her forehead.

The metal burned against her skin, the acrid smell of gunpowder stung as it drifted into her nostrils. Still on her knees, she faced Shaun and looked past him to Logan who lay curled on his side, blood oozing onto his white coat from a gunshot wound. Tears began rolling down her cheeks, "No," she cried, closing her eyes to the horrific scene. "Logan, no." He didn't move or draw a breath.   "Logan!"   she screamed only to be met with a backhand and a command to shut up.

She watched as Logan still lay motionless on the cold tile floor, eyes open and mouth parted slightly. There'd been no reaction to her scream. His lifeless body collapsed near the wall, his arm draped across his stomach, his eyes trained on her.

Sydney felt the life melt from her. The blood settled cold in her veins, her heart slowed to a dull, negligible pace. Every beat overflowed with grief and pain. The agony of losing her true love ripped the soul from her. She'd never known a more thoroughly debilitating anguish in her life. Physical pain couldn't compare to it. She couldn't see it or touch it but she could feel it and it was unbearable.

Images of their brief time together flooded her brain. Of the love they declared for each other, of the love they openly shared. In her mind, she saw his mouth tipped in that gorgeous smile, felt his strong arms, heard his deep voice reassuring her. Other memories floated in now, of feeling safe in his embrace, of his promises to love and protect her. He'd done both. Even at the last, he protected her and had done his best to save her.

She opened her eyes to see Ethan crouched next to Logan, his focus switching from checking Logan's wound to following Shaun's movements.

Sydney begged for visual reassurance of Logan's condition but Ethan gave no indication. No nod, no shake of the head. Nothing. Seeing Logan's powerful, lively form now lying silent and motionless on the floor was too much to bear. "Logan," she called through her tears, reaching for him.

Shaun shoved her back on her heels and glanced back at Logan and Ethan. Ethan held pressure to Logan's wound somewhere beneath the once pristine white coat but Logan still didn't move.

A swell of heartache boiled up in her throat until it found freedom. Sydney dissolved in tears, her face buried in her hands. Jason warned her she'd endanger Logan if she interfered. She didn't just endanger him, she got him killed. She'd never be able to live with that fact.

A swift and brutal pain across her cheek propelled her to the floor. Shaun aimed the .45 straight at her, "Shut up!"

Alarmed, Ethan visually tried to discourage her from disobeying. Shaun's backhand should have registered more but she hadn't outwardly reacted. She was too emotionally numb.

The tears continued falling as the scene of Logan's lifeless body branded itself in her brain. She couldn't live without Logan. She did, however, want revenge for him. Sydney vowed to die avenging Logan's death and along with it, she could save Ethan.

Through tears of misery, she clenched her teeth, "I lied. I am a cop." She balled her fist and swung, hoping to knock the gun from his hand.

The announcement both surprised and horrified Ethan. He pleaded, "Sydney, *don't*,"

A swell of pure molten wrath surged through Shaun as he caught her hand, twisted and shoved her face first to the floor.

Throwing her hands out to cushion her landing, she turned to face Logan. She was the last person he saw before he died, and he would be her last.

From the corner of her vision, she saw Shaun raise the gun until it pressed against her cheek. Then she saw Ethan scramble to his feet. He would try to save her but could now save himself. With her distraction, he could easily overpower Shaun. With a solid kick, Ethan knocked the gun's aim from Sydney as Shaun pulled the trigger. The shot exploded in her ears and she cried out from fear and pain. As close as the blast sounded, it took a moment to realize Ethan deflected the shot away.

Then movement diverted her vision. She blinked, unsure of what she'd just witnessed. Through her tear-filled vision, everything moved in slow motion as Logan magically levered himself to his feet, his eyes darting alertly now, and they focused on her, "Get out now!"

She froze, thoroughly stunned. She couldn't believe her eyes as his spirited form joined Ethan in battle, "Logan?" Though he faked his death, the blood was real and it still oozed from a wound in his arm. He had been shot but was alive. *Alive.* So alive his voice sounded like a field commander in war, "Damn it, Sydney, listen to me and run!" He hurled his good fist into Shaun's kidney and as the young man flailed to protect himself, Logan launched his fist into his stomach. Both brothers fought

for the gun Shaun carelessly wielded while squeezing off rounds, hoping
to shoot anyone near him. Finally Ethan wrapped his hand around
Shaun's wrist to control the direction of the shots.

Sydney crawled behind the cabinet to hide. Her heart still wasn't beating
correctly and she still felt dizzy. The crushing blow of thinking Logan
was dead then suddenly realizing it was merely an act made her weak all
over again. He could have been killed trying to save her – and she
thought he had been.

She peeked around the corner to see both brothers tackle Shaun,
Ethan finally pried the weapon loose while Logan injected a fast-acting
sedative. Logan administered the drug with the tenderness of a Nazi,
jabbing the needle into Shaun's arm. Sydney heard a yelp from Shaun as
Logan injected the medication. Ethan pushed his hand back, "Easy, bro.
He's gotta go to trial. Helps if he's alive to do it."

Releasing the ferocity he'd contained for hours, Logan growled,
"The bastard should have thought of that before he hit Sydney."

Sydney felt faint. Despite her shaking limbs, she pushed herself
upright to her knees as Logan appeared, his long legs engulfing her
vision. Sensing her exhaustion, his large hands reached down to bring
her into his embrace. He winced from the pressure on his arm, "You
okay, sweetheart?"

Barely able to answer, she nodded, "I thought you were dead,"
she managed before allowing a river of tears to flow. He held her quietly,
stroking her hair, "That would have been terribly rude on my part. After
all, we have a date tonight and I'd never miss that."

Sydney laughed, the sound emerging shaky but joyfully as she clung to him. He pulled away, tipping her chin back to meet his gaze, "I did, however, make a promise to myself today."

"What promise?"

His eyes glittered with a sinfulness she last saw that morning, "To teach you a lesson about going into harm's way. You, sweetheart, are going over my knee the second we get home. Once I think you've learned your lesson, you're mine for the whole night."

"I'm yours forever," she corrected with a smile. Logan pulled her back into his embrace and she savored his nearness and the feeling of his arms around her.

Ethan continued talking on the phone, "Inform Grady and Crawford Long we need ambulances and advise Chief Brown our temporary recruit is shaken up but is still her same obstinate self." Ethan hung up and the doors burst open with a flood of police and Sydney took a moment to notice the rain had stopped. The thunder ceased as well as the torrential rain. It was as if Mother Nature sensed the danger had passed and a ray of sun split the clouds, brightening the streets again. Ethan approached Sydney's back, announcing gruffly, "You're never allowed in a hostage rescue again and don't even *think* about becoming a cop."

Sydney sniffed back her tears and looked at him, joking, "Afraid you'll have to address me as 'ma'am' someday?"

Ethan's arms suddenly opened and enveloped her in a bear hug, "No, it's because if anything happened to you, I don't think I'd live through it."

"I definitely second that emotion," Logan agreed, wrapping them both in a hug of his own.

Epilogue

The dinner party broke up shortly after eight. Ethan and Logan leaned back, stuffed full of the honey-pecan chicken and German chocolate sheet cake. Ethan patted his stomach, "Nice dinner, Syd. Tasted a lot like Ma's cooking."

"Told you she had the knack," Logan winked then sipped his wine. He poured himself a little more then tilted the bottle toward Sydney's glass.

"Yeah, well, you're biased," his brother countered. He toyed with his napkin, painstakingly folding it into a duck. His ability to fold the wings just so and make the tail flair upward engrossed the group.

Samantha arched her brow with interest as Ethan waddled the miniature duck toward her. She took it and examined it, trying to figure out how he folded it. "Ethan, you need a hobby."

He pushed his chair out a bit, "Climb onto Ethan's lap. You'll like his hobby."

Sydney stifled a laugh while Logan slapped him with his napkin, telling him to behave. Sam sported her best affronted expression, "You never cease to surprise me."

"Good," he shot a glance at Sydney. "At least I can surprise one of you girls." Now he sneered at Sydney who sneered back.

"Now children," Logan gently scolded, "play nice."

Sydney's brow sank but replied good-naturedly, "If I'm a child, you're going to jail, buddy."

"Think our plans might be jeopardized?" he inquired.

The comment raised Sam's interest and she asked what plans. Logan and Sydney reached under the table, their vision never straying from each other. Sam and Ethan watched curiously as the two smiled then Sydney unexpectedly jumped then giggled.

"For the love of God," Ethan blushed while burying his face in his hands, "save it for the bedroom, you two."

He heard Samantha gasp and reflected how sweet that sounded. The ice queen awakens. Then her voice gushed, "Oh my God, Syd. Oh, Ethan, look."

Oh, Ethan... Did she have to say it so breathlessly? So... so sensually? Ethan suddenly felt a stirring in his trousers. His body's reaction appeared in more than his khakis. The surprise was etched into his expression. He locked on Samantha allowing wicked thoughts to race between his ears.

Sam glanced up and stopped, halted by his heated gaze. Without breaking eye contact, she swallowed and pointed, "Look."

Ethan forced his vision to Sydney. He felt his jaw drop. "You're getting married?"

Nodding, Logan took Sydney's hand, held it. Meanwhile, Ethan stared blankly at the diamond perched on Sydney's left hand. *Nice rock… Big one, too.* The modest rock set in white gold should have pissed him off. It should have shaken him so fiercely that jealousy boiled in his throat – just like it always had concerning Sydney but all he felt was horny. He wanted to jump Sydney's sister right there on the dining table in front of all creation.

He laid a hand across his forehead. No, no fever. He took a quick physical inventory of his body. Everything was in perfect working order and he felt fine except the boner in his shorts. Samantha? Why *Samantha?* He cringed, convinced he'd lost his mind and was close to losing his control.

"Ethan?" Sydney called quietly. "Are you okay?"

Her voice brought his vision to her concerned features. Then he smiled. *Oh , what the hell…* A laugh bubbled from deep inside and found freedom, much to everyone's shock. He laughed until his stomach hurt and tears fell down his cheeks. While the group waited for his decorum to return, he wiped his cheeks with a napkin and answered, "I think it's great, guys. Congratulations."

A collective sigh filled the room. Sam's enthusiasm bloomed full force as she admired the diamond on her sister's hand, "Oh, Syd. I *knew* you two were up to something tonight." Her smile widened, "It's beautiful, honey. Congratulations to both of you."

"Thanks, Samantha." Logan squeezed Sydney's hand.

"Don't thank me yet, brother-in-law. You still haven't told our parents. If you survive that," she cocked an eyebrow at Sydney, "you're home free."

"Eh," Ethan waved it off, "they'll be fine. Their girl's marrying a doctor, for God's sake." He turned his attention to Samantha, "She just traded handcuff fantasies for playing doctor."

Logan swatted the side of his head, "That's my wife you're talking about."

Sam stood up, winking, "And I'll bet these two want to celebrate their engagement." She began gathering empty plates, "Ethan, get up and help."

"God, woman, you're so bossy," he swallowed the rest of his wine. When he stood, he carefully maneuvered so no one saw his raging hard-on. For some reason, Sam's nearness gave him stone aches. Her voice made his gut hard as a rock, and his heart race.

Sam threw an incredulous glance over her shoulder, "Sydney and Logan cooked, the least we can do is clean up for them."

Ethan nearly groaned at how sweet she looked now. Why hadn't he noticed earlier? Her eyes the color of sapphire swept across his vision like a soft touch. Grinning, he chided, "*They* invited *us*, remember?" He laughed while ducking Sam's playful slap.   "Ethan,   you surprise me," Logan mentioned. "We were both afraid of your reaction."

"Oh hell, Syd's too wild for me. She takes too many chances like nearly getting her ass shot off. You're in for a hell of a life, bro. Mark my words." He nudged Sydney's chair as he passed, "I need a more settled woman."

"Sam's available," Sydney remarked. Ethan wondered if she sensed his longing from across the table. When she touched his arm and winked, he knew she had.

"Don't even joke about that, Syd." Sam called from the kitchen,

"Cats and dogs, that's Ethan and me."

Sydney and Logan both saw Ethan's shoulders instantly droop. He trudged around the table while rolling his sleeves back. Grabbing plates and glasses, he sighed. He was losing hope fast.

Sydney tossed her crumpled napkin at him. It thwacked his head and she whispered, "Don't give up."

Ethan's brow sank with mischievousness. He tossed the napkin back, "Put you over my knee, little girl."

"That's my job, Ethan." Logan corrected him then turned to Sydney, "And I take my job *very* seriously." He leaned back in his chair, addressing Sam, "Even cats and dogs get along sometimes, Samantha."

Ethan stopped at the kitchen door. Holding a load of dirty dishes, he turned back with not only a wicked gleam in his eyes but plenty of wicked fantasies playing in his mind. "She *would* be a handful, wouldn't she?"

"Go for it, bro. She can only say no."

He shrugged, "And slam a frying pan across my nose. But what the hell, why not try?" He thumped the back of Sydney's chair with his foot, "See? You didn't get rid of me after all." The smile returned as he strolled confidently into the kitchen, "Hey, Sam, what're you doing Friday?"

Logan chuckled as his brother chanced asking Samantha out. Clear surprise lifted her tone, "Why, Ethan Calhoun, are you asking me for a date?"

Ethan hemmed and hawed for a reply. Logan imagined him toeing the tile floor like a self-conscious kid. "Yes," Logan answered for his brother, "that's what he's doing."

In his mind he envisioned Samantha crossing her arms and leaning against the cabinet when she asked, "And where do you want to take me on this date? To the Burger Hut?"

Ethan never spoke a word. Instead Logan tossed out a suggestion, "How about an actual restaurant where you have menus, Ethan? Sam might like that."

"You're darn tootin' I would," Sydney's sister concurred.

Ethan finally found his voice, "Then you choose where. You're always in charge anyway. Just make sure I can afford the joint, will ya? Cops don't make that much."

"I know just the place."

Ethan's reply was low and muffled but Sam's sudden laugh told Logan his brother wasn't a total lost cause with women. Her voice also lowered to a secretive whisper, "After we wash up these dishes, let's go see a movie. Want to?"

Logan heard his brother begin to stammer. The situation careened out of control for him – which the older brother expected. Samantha never sat back and let things happen, she *made* them happen. Ethan ultimately squeezed a reluctant "u-huh" from his paralyzed lips. Dishes clattered and clanked as Sam started rinsing them, "I'll be ready in about twenty minutes."

Logan listened to the banter for a minute then he reached out, touched Sydney's cheek. His fingers trailed down her shoulder to her hand.   Toying with the diamond, he tugged her closer, "What're *you* doing in twenty minutes?"

She brushed his lips with hers, "I'm thinking of going to bed early. Join me?"

He smiled, "Meet you there." Then kissed her again, "We'll do some undercover work of our own."

J.L. Lemon lives in Texas surrounded by a loving and supportive family, two adorable and devoted puppies, and hordes of garden gnomes.

Before 2002, J.L. Lemon wrote opinions and product reviews for an online consumer guide. When fellow reviewers cited the author's knack for humor, she decided to return to writing fiction. Along with Second Chances, she's published 5 books in the Savannah Stories Series with 3 more in the works. For more titles from J.L. Lemon, please visit:

www.geocities.com/upatmidnightpublishing
www.geocities.com/authorjllemon